TEN AND A KID

TEN
AND A KID

SADIE ROSE WEILERSTEIN

PICTURES BY JANINA DOMANSKA

The Jewish Publication Society
of America
Philadelphia

CONTENTS

To
MAMA AND PAPA
IN LOVING AND GRATEFUL MEMORY

" LOOK TO THE ROCK
WHENCE YOU WERE HEWN."
ISAIAH 51, VERSE 1.

TEN AND A KID

Introducing the Family

THIS IS THE LITTLE TOWN, far across the sea in
Lithuania, where the family lived. It was a very old
town. You can see the hole in the square where the
cobblestones have worn away. 11

This is their street, very muddy, with just four houses. Theirs is the little one that looks as if it had been picked up by its roof and stuck into a mud puddle. The two rooms *inside* are clean and cheerful. Every spring the walls and the big clay oven are whitewashed. Every Friday the floor is sprinkled with fresh yellow sand.

12

And here is the family.

Avrom Itsik

his good wife Gittel
The children called her Momme

their six daughters—

Esther, the eldest,
going on fifteen

Fayge, twelve

Goldie, ten

Reizel, eight

Teppele and Tseppele, the twins, six

and Kezele, the only
brother, four years old

Later there will be another brother,
Dovidel, the baby

Also a little white kid, Gadya

This is as good a time as any to tell you about the names. Sometimes Esther was called Esterel, Fayge, Faygele, Goldie, Goldele, and Reizel, Reizele, just as one says Tommy or Johnny.

Teppele, Tseppele and Kezele were nicknames, not real names. Hardly anyone called the little ones by their real names, so there is no use remembering them.

Kezele means little cheese, Tseppele little braid, and Teppele, little pot.

Do you see the shirt tail sticking out of the slit in the back of Kezele's trousers? It was the shirt tail that gave him his name. His sisters were always tucking it back where it belonged, but out it came again. It looked to them like a little heart shaped cheese, a *kezele*. So they called little brother Kezele after his shirt tail.

Tseppele's real name was Tsippe. She was called Tseppele because of her braids, *tsep*. They weren't long, well behaved braids like Esther's and Fayge's. They were short and thin and danced behind her. One could not help calling a Tsippele with dancing braids Tseppele.

But Teppele, Little Pot! Why should Teppele be called a pot? Some said it was because she was round and roly-poly like a pot. Some said it was because she was always sticking her head into Momme's pot to see what was in it. Teppele's roly-poly stomach never was full. Some said it was to rhyme with Tseppele.

Teppele
Tseppele

It was fitting for twins' names to rhyme.

Now you have met the whole family, those already here and those who are still to come.

We are ready to begin.

Pesach Is Coming

MELTING SNOW HAD TURNED the hole in the cobblestones into a gleaming mirror. Reizel, crossing the square, stopped to look down into it. She saw a bright-eyed, red-cheeked Reizel with not much of a nose, a pointy chin, and a kerchief tied under the chin.

A breeze stirred the water. Now Reizel saw two noses, three chins. She stuck out her tongue at Reizel-in-the-water to see how many tongues she could give her. The breeze moved on. The water grew still. It mirrored a deep blue sky and fluffy clouds, very white clouds, very clean, as if they had just been scrubbed for Passover. The clouds reminded Reizel of her message. Off she went, across the square to the lane. Up went her skirts and her red flannel petticoat as she jumped over a mud puddle. On the doorstep she scraped her feet impatiently, then burst inside.

"Momme, Momme, the new flour is in! Sarah Beile, the baker woman, says will you tell her when you want to bake your *matza*."

"*Matza!*" Six excited voices caught up the word.

The time had come to bake *matza*, unleavened bread. *Matza* meant the coming of Passover, the beloved festival that celebrated the going out from bondage in Egypt. It meant going to the cobbler to

19

be measured for new shoes. It meant different foods, and different dishes, and the *seder* which was both solemn service and joyful feast.

"Can we bake *matza* next week, Momme?"

"Will you talk to Sarah Beile tomorrow, Momme?"

"Why can't we bake our *matza* this week, Momme?"

Father's voice broke in drily.

"A small matter stands in the way. The new flour is in, but the money to buy the flour is not yet in."

"It will come," said Momme quietly. "Has it failed us yet at the *Pesach* season?"

The children looked at Momme gratefully.

The very next Friday Father entered the house with a broad smile on his face.

"Well, Gittel," he said, "have you set a day to bake *matza?* The flour is bought."

"Where did you get the money, Father?" Reizel asked.

"Where do you suppose?" said Father. "Elijah the prophet gave it to me."

Reizel looked at Father in astonishment. True, the good prophet still wandered about the earth, helping people in their need as he had once helped the poor widow in the Bible. But who would have thought her own father would meet him? It seemed too wonderful to believe. A gleam in Father's eyes told Reizel that it *was* too wonderful to believe.

20

"You're teasing me," she said.

"Of course," said Father. "Who am I that the prophet should come to me? In a lucky hour I bought a load of hides, and in a lucky hour I sold them at a good price. Our Passover is provided for."

On an appointed day Momme and Father presented themselves at the bakery. All the children were with them, eyes eager, hands scrubbed and rescrubbed that there might be no trace of leaven. Father said that leaven was not only bread that had risen. It was everything stale and unclean.

The family followed the baker into a long, high-ceilinged room. New boards had been laid across trestles to form a table. At one end stood the sack of new flour and a barrel of water, drawn from the well the day before. Work began at once. The baker's helper mixed flour and water into dough. Momme cut off a piece and handed it to Esther, who rolled it flat and passed it to Fayge, who ran a little wheel across it, puncturing it with small holes. The little ones ran back and forth carrying the dough cakes from the table to the oven. Everyone took turns at helping, even Teppele and Tseppele, who were not much taller than they were round and had to stand on stools to reach the table.

"Hurry! Fast!" Father urged the workers on. "The dough will get warm. It will rise."

His daughters did not need the reminder. They knew how important it was to keep the dough from

21

rising. Their *matzas* must be exactly like the ones the Children of Israel ate when they went in haste out of Egypt—flat, without leaven or salt.

Reizel thought about the Children of Israel as she watched the round crisp *matzas* come out of the oven. Father had told her that the Children of Israel had complained to Moses because there were no leeks and onions in the wilderness. She guessed they wanted to eat the onions with their *matza. Matza* was delicious spread with goose fat and onions. Reizel knew that she should be ashamed of the Children of Israel for being so greedy. Yet she sympathized with them.

"Reizel is dreaming again! Wake up Reizel."

Goldie's voice brought Reizel back to the bakery. Momme was wrapping the batches of *matza* in clean white cloths. Carefully she set them into a basket.

"May you have a joyful and *kosher Pesach,* Sarah Beile," Momme wished the baker woman.

"You also, Gittel," said the baker woman.

She looked thoughtfully at the six little sisters, then added, "May you live to see each lovely daughter a queen at her own *seder* table."

A smile lighted Momme's face.

"From your lips to God's ears," she said.

Then the family set out for home.

Hannah Rachel Tells a Story

"LOOK, MOMME, HANNAH RACHEL has begun her *Pesach* cleaning."

Reizel pointed to a table and stools piled in front of the door of Hannah Rachel, their neighbor.

"When will we take down the *Pesachdig* dishes, Momme?"

There was so much to be done. Every corner of the house must be cleaned and scrubbed, the year-round dishes put away, Passover plates and bowls brought out, metal spoons and knives used all the year purified in a cauldron of boiling water, copper pots taken to the tinsmith to be relined. Not the tiniest bit of leaven must remain in the house on Passover.

But Momme was not the hurrying kind.

"We'll sit down at the *seder* at the same time as everyone else," she would say when the children pressed her, an answer which satisfied none of them, least of all Reizel.

Reizel had a special reason for her impatience. The reason went back to the day she stopped in at Hannah

Rachel's house and found her taking down a large silver wine cup, an Elijah cup. Father also had an Elijah cup, though not a silver one. Was not Elijah invited to every Jewish home on Passover Eve? At a certain point in the service his cup was filled with wine, and the door opened wide for him to enter.

Now Reizel learned of another way to make the prophet welcome. Hannah Rachel told her that in the village where she was born, a distant village hidden among steep mountains, they not only filled a cup for Elijah, they set a chair for him at the *seder* table.

Reizel looked puzzled. One did not *see* Elijah on *seder* night. To tell whether he had entered you had to watch his cup. If the wine went down, Elijah had drunk of it. But how could one tell whether an invisible one had sat in a chair?

Hannah Rachel explained. "When Elijah stays long enough to sit in a chair, he does not come unseen. He comes disguised as a stranger."

Then she told Reizel the story of the pious water carrier.

"There lived in our town," Hannah Rachel said, "a poor water carrier of great piety. Shmuel was his name, and the name of his wife was Breindel. It happened on a *seder* night that Shmuel had just recited, 'Let all who are hungry come and eat,' when there was a knock on the door. A stranger stood outside. He carried a beggar's sack, but his manner was not that of a beggar.

"Shmuel welcomed him. Breindel led him to the *seder* table.

"'The good prophet will not mind if we give his seat to a poor wanderer,' Breindel thought, as she seated the stranger in Elijah's chair.

"The stranger *was* Elijah," Reizel interrupted excitedly.

"Who else?" said Hannah Rachel. "But the good couple did not know this until the end of the *seder*. The guest joined in the service, ate and drank with them. Breindel could not help wishing she had more fitting food to offer. God in his goodness had sent them a guest for the *seder*, and what did she serve him? Eggs and plain beet *borsht* with potatoes!

"Breindel's thoughts turned to the foods she would have liked to serve: tender chicken, maybe goose; golden chicken soup; in the soup the *knaedlach* she knew so well how to make but made so seldom, *matza*-meal balls rich with fat and with eggs. Each would have an extra globule of fat in the center. 'A *knaedel* with a soul,' Shmuel called it.

"Mind you, Breindel did not *say* this. She only thought it, so that it startled her to have the stranger ask, 'Where is it written that one must eat *knaedlach* and fowl at the *seder?*'

"Then he praised the *borsht,* calling it a royal dish of a royal color. As for the eggs, there was that in their taste, he said, which reminded one of the offerings in the Holy Temple.

"Moreover, he spiced the meal with tales of distant places and strange customs, and of the beauties of the Holy Land. He was speaking of the sparks of holiness that were hidden in all things, even in common things, when Breindel brought the tea to the table. Now you must know that whenever Breindel set a glass of tea on the table, a longing came over her— longing for a piece of white sugar. Not for herself! For her Shmuel. The sugar would rest on his tongue while the hot tea flowed through it, absorbing its sweetness. On Passover one saw great cones of white sugar in rich folk's homes. The thought of them brought a sigh to Breindel's lips.

"The sigh passed quickly. It was time to begin the second part of the service."

Again Reizel interrupted the story.

"Hannah Rachel," she asked, "didn't they even *guess* that the stranger was Elijah?"

"No," said Hannah Rachel, "not until they came to 'How Many Are the Wonders God Has Wrought by Night.'

"Shmuel always sang this song with special feeling. He shut his eyes, centering all his thoughts on God's mercies. His voice was like a bird, mounting up and up into the heavens to pour out its thanks.

"All through the singing Breindel's eyes were fixed on her husband. She thought, 'How blessed I am to have a husband who can read the holy prayers, and has, moreover, a voice like an angel's.' She considered his goodness, how every day he rose before dawn to carry water to lame Yudel and the widow Zlote and her orphans before going on his rounds. He did this even in the bitter cold of winter. More than once she had put salve on his hands where the icy rope had cut into them.

"Breindel was so busy with her thoughts, she did not know that the song had ended until a cry from Shmuel startled her. He was pointing to Elijah's chair. *The chair was empty!*

"On the table in front of it something glowed, and sparkled, and sent forth rays of light.

"It was a *cone of white sugar.* Not an ordinary cone! This cone had in it the brightness of a thousand diamonds.

"Then Shmuel and Breindel knew that their guest

29

had been the prophet Elijah. He had read Breindel's thoughts and given her her heart's desire."

"But Hannah Rachel," Reizel asked, "what of Shmuel's heart's desire?"

"Foolish one," said Hannah Rachel. "Shmuel's desire was that Breindel might have her heart's desire."

Out of Hannah Rachel's story came Reizel's plan. She, too, would set a chair for Elijah. He might come to their *seder* as he had come to the water carrier's.

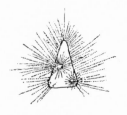

A Gift from Elijah

PASSOVER EVE CAME at last. Everything was ready, just as Momme had said. Momme's candles gleamed on the *matza,* the wine filled cups, on the *haggadahs,* old and wine-stained, the prayer books from which the service was to be read. Round the table sat the children in their holiday best.

Father was called a king on *seder* night. But he looked more like a high priest as he sat at the head of the table in his long white festival robe, arranging the symbols for the service: three *matzas* wrapped in a linen cover; on the *matzas* the *seder* plate; in the plate, a shankbone in remembrance of the paschal lamb, a roast egg in mourning for the Holy Temple, greens for the springtime, bitter herbs to remind them how bitter it was to be a slave, *haroses* that looked like the mortar the Children of Israel mixed in the brickyards of Egypt. Luckily the *haroses* did not taste like mortar. It was made of chopped apples and nuts and wine and tasted delicious. There was also a bowl of salt water, as salty as the tears of the slaves.

Now that all was in order, Father looked around at the children. Four of them were crowded on a single bench. Yet the high-backed chair was vacant.

Reizel hastened to explain.

31

"The chair is for Elijah, Father. Hannah Rachel says where she comes from a chair is placed for Elijah. If you invite a guest you should prepare a chair for him."

"Do you think Elijah will have time to sit down," Father asked, "with all the homes he must visit tonight?"

Reizel held her breath.

Would Father laugh at her and tell Esther to move over into the vacant chair?

No! He lifted his cup of wine. The service had begun. First the *kiddush,* the blessing of the festival. Thanks to God who created the fruit of the vine and had given them this holy festival for happiness and rejoicing. Thanks to God who had kept them in life and cared for them and enabled them to reach this season!

Each one took his first sip of wine. Esther and Fayge brought Father a pitcher of water and a basin so that he might wash his hands. Now bits of the sprouting green onions were passed around, and God was thanked for creating the "fruit of the earth." The "fruit of the earth," dipped in salt water, had a sharp, delicious taste.

Next Father broke the middle *matza* in two, wrapped half of it in a napkin, and hid it under a pillow to be saved for dessert. Then he lifted the remaining *matza* high.

"Let all who are hungry come and eat. Let all who

are downcast come and celebrate the Passover with us."

Reizel's eyes turned toward the door. This was the moment of which she had been dreaming. She knew exactly what would happen. The door would open and a stranger would enter, an old man with a flowing beard, a wanderer's staff in his hand. He would sit down at the table. The chair was waiting for him. His voice would rise with the sweetness of King David's harp. Only she, Reizel, would know that this was Elijah. Suddenly, at the close of the *seder,* he would disappear, leaving behind him . . .

Reizel could not think just what he would leave behind. In the stories it was a cone of sugar, or *matza* and wine, or a fine fowl. But, thanks to the Highest One, they already had *matza* and wine and *matza* meal and eggs, and a fowl, and goose fat, even a cone of white sugar. True, the sugar did not sparkle with the brightness of the water carrier's cone. But when you hammered it into bits and kept a bit on the tongue, it melted with a delicious sweetness. God himself had provided them with their needs, enough for the whole eight days of Passover.

Kezele's voice, high and excited, broke into Reizel's dreaming.

"Father," he was saying, "I will ask you four questions."

Reizel looked up with a start. Elijah's chair was still empty. The only guest at the table was Mume

Bryna, Reb Baruch's widow, and she had been there
from the beginning. All eyes were on Kezele.

"*Ma-nish-ta-nah ha-lai-lah ha-zeh,* wherefore is this
night, *mi-kol ha-lei-los,* different from all other nights,"
recited Kezele, his voice rising and falling in the
customary chant.

The sisters listened tensely, repeating the words
under their breath. They were more relieved than
Kezele when the last question had been properly
asked.

"Now I will give you your answer," Father said.
Again he took up the chant. "*Avodim hayeenu*—slaves
were we unto Pharaoh in the land of Egypt and the
Lord our God brought us forth . . ." He read, not in
their everyday speech, which was Yiddish, but in
Hebrew, the holy tongue.

Reizel went back to her dreaming. Elijah's chair
was vacant, but he might yet come—in the second
half of the *seder* when they opened the door for him.
She should not have expected him so early. Did he
not have homes in all the lands of the world to visit,
in far Russia, and Germany, and the land beyond the
Sambatyan River, and America?

Reizel's thoughts went wandering with Elijah.

The first part of the *seder* was over. They had said
the proper blessings and eaten the proper foods:
bitter herbs dipped in sweet *haroses;* bitter herbs be-

tween pieces of *matza;* hard-boiled eggs in salt water; delicious chicken soup with circles of fat, "golden eyes," floating on the top; *matza* meal balls that melted in the mouth.

Now Father was reciting the grace after meals.

Reizel's eyes turned to the vacant chair. Soon, soon Elijah would take his place there. His cup was already filled with wine.

"Who will open the door?" Father asked.

"I'll open it. Let me open it."

Reizel was out of her seat and at the door before Father could answer.

The night air felt soft and cool against her cheeks. Songs floated through the darkness. A full moon silvered the house tops.

"Come, Elijah, please come! I have set a chair for you," Reizel whispered. Then, fearful that she had been too bold, she added, "Maybe you are too busy to stay. Then come unseen as you always do. Only leave a sign."

Had something brushed past her in the darkness, something white and cloudlike?

"You can shut the door now. Father has finished," said Momme.

It made no difference which child opened the door on *seder* night. Momme was always close behind. Now Momme bolted the door carefully.

At the table the children were bending over Elijah's cup.

35

"He came," said Kezele. "I saw the wine go down."

"It only wiggled. Goldie pushed the table," Tseppele insisted.

"Hush," said Esther.

Reizel wasn't listening. Her eyes were on Elijah's chair. *The chair was vacant.* Elijah had left no sign.

"Out of my distress, I called upon the Lord," Father chanted.

The melody had a sadness in it like Reizel's own thoughts.

Suddenly the singing changed to a joyous *Halleluyah.*

"Our Passover service is over and done," Father concluded.

But the *seder* was not done. There were songs to be sung.

> *Who knows one?*
> *I know One.*
> *One is God who made Heaven and Earth.*
> *Who knows two?*

Question, answer! Question, answer! The words tripped over each other, faster and faster, joyous, eager, verse piled on verse. Father led, the children followed—all but Kezele. Kezele had fallen asleep, his head resting in his arms on the table.

"I'll carry him to bed," said Momme.

"Not now," Esther pleaded.

She shook little brother gently.

"Wake up, Kezele. It's time for 'Had Gadya.'"

It would not do for Kezele to miss "Had Gadya," the final song, the crown of all the songs.

> *"An only kid, one only kid*
> *My father bought for two zuzim.*
> *Then came a cat and ate the kid*
> *My father bought for two zuzim."*

On and on went the song. Dog bit cat, stick beat dog, fire burned stick.

The verses grew longer and longer, coming at last to a triumphant end.

"Then came the Holy One, Blessed be He, and slew Death's Angel that had slain the butcher, that had slaughtered the ox, that had drunk the water, that had quenched the fire, that had burned the stick, that had beaten the dog, that had bit the cat, that had eaten the kid, that my father bought for two zuzim—

> *Had Gadya*
> *Had Gadya*
> *One only kid!"*

The children ended breathlessly, all eyes on Father.

Suddenly they heard a plaintive, shivery maa-aa-a.

Reizel turned. A kid was standing on Elijah's chair, a tiny snow-white kid.

Had Gadya!

The cat had eaten it. Dog, stick, fire, water, ox, slaughterer, the very Angel of Death—all had been

37

caught up in its misfortune. And here it was, sound and whole at their *seder* table.

How had it come about? Where had the kid come from?

"From out of doors," said Father. "Is there a shortage of goats in our town? It must have wandered in when Reizel opened the door for Elijah."

Elijah! Of all Father's words Reizel caught up this one. Of course! *Elijah* had brought the kid. He had heard her prayer and left a sign.

A commotion interrupted her thoughts. The tiny kid had jumped on the table. Its pink nose was poking at a *haggadah*. Reizel grabbed the kid in her arms, but not before it had upset a wine cup.

"It wanted to read in the *haggadah*," said Kezele, now wide-awake.

"It wanted to *eat* the *haggadah*," said Father.

Momme came to the kid's defense.

"Did you offer it other food?" she asked. "Who was it that said: 'Let all who are hungry come and eat'?"

Momme, too, could quote a passage when she wanted to.

The leftover greens were gathered up, and the kid coaxed to the center of the room. All the family gathered round to watch it eat.

Suddenly, with the last bite, the little kid jumped up on its hind legs and began to dance. Its ears flopped, its stubby tail wagged, its forepaws swayed.

Father took hold of Kezele's hand. Kezele grabbed
Esther. Goldie, Reizel, Teppele, Tseppele, the whole
family joined in the dance. Even Momme and old
Mume Bryna were drawn in. Round and round the
little kid they circled, singing,

> *Had-gad-yoh! Had-gad-yoh!*
> *One only kid! One only kid!*

Next morning Father inquired of all the neighbors. None of them had lost a kid. He had the sexton make an announcement in the synagogue. Throughout the Passover week the family kept looking for the owner. In vain! At the end of the festival they knew no more than at the beginning.

"I told you," said Reizel. "*Elijah* brought the kid. Wasn't it standing in Elijah's chair?"

"I have some questions in my mind about that," said Father, "but we will save them for Elijah to answer." It is Elijah who will answer all unanswered questions in the time to come.

So the little white kid remained with the family. They named him Had Gadya, which was soon shortened to Gadya.

"Do you know what I think, Gadya?" Reizel said, hugging him. "I think you *are* Had Gadya. I think you didn't die, but went up to heaven like Elijah. Now Elijah has brought you to us."

A sudden thought set her heart dancing. Elijah worked wonders. Maybe his kid would work wonders.

Anything might happen.

Without-Fish with Fish

SOMETHING DID HAPPEN. Two weeks after Passover, a new baby wrapped in swaddling clothes, a little brother, Dovidel, lay in the cradle beside Momme's bed. Under the cradle lay Gadya like the kid in the lullaby.

> Under my child's cradle,
> Rests a snow-white kid.

Reizel suggested that the kid might have had something to do with the coming of the baby, but others laughed the idea away. Hadn't they known even before *Pesach* that Momme was to have the baby?

So Reizel waited for another wonder to happen, and before Momme was strong enough to leave the bed, one did. It wasn't a big wonder like the splitting of the Red Sea. But it was big enough for the children, especially Teppele.

Teppele and Tseppele, you remember, were twins. Both were roly-poly. Both had short thin braids. But there was a difference. With Tseppele, it was the braids that danced. With Teppele, it was her tongue. Teppele's tongue was never still. Either she was eating, or she was talking about eating.

Not that her stomach was overfilled. It couldn't be in Avrom Itsik's house—except with potatoes. Potatoes grew in their garden. Momme served them boiled, with a bit of salt herring and a big spoonful of herring juice. She grated them raw, and fried them into crisp pancakes. Several times a week she served a dish that they called without-fish. Without-fish had everything in it that goes into the making of boiled fish—potatoes, an onion, salt, pepper, a little milk—everything, that is, except the fish. That was why it was called without-fish. Teppele would eat her portion to the last bit, sopping up the milky sauce with a piece of bread.

"Good," she would say, rubbing her stomach. "But it would be better to have without-fish *with* fish."

Now you are ready to hear about the wonder. It began when Kezele decided to take a ride on Gadya. He grabbed hold of the little kid and began climbing on his back. But Gadya wasn't like the sisters who always let Kezele have his own way. Up went his legs, down went his head, and the astonished Kezele was on the floor. Fayge ran to pick him up. Goldie said it was all Gadya's fault. Reizel sprang to his defense. Esther tried to hush them.

"Sh, sh," she kept saying. "You'll wake the baby."

It was too late. The baby was already awake. From the bedroom came Momme's voice, "Children, what's wrong?"

"Nothing," Esther assured her, looking in at the door. "Try to go to sleep, Momme. I'm taking the children to the lake."

She closed the door carefully, and turned to the children.

"Who wants to go to the lake with me? I have some things to wash."

All the children wanted to go. Down the lane they went, their bare feet splashing in the mud puddles. Gadya danced beside them. Esther carried a few underthings to wash out in the lake.

The sky was deep blue and the lake as blue as the sky. Suddenly Teppele pointed excitedly. Something was sparkling on the water, close to the bank. It wasn't the sun. At least, it wasn't just the sun. The sparkles were moving. Little shadows darted in and out among them. Esther dropped the clothes in the grass and stooped down over the water. She saw hundreds and hundreds of tiny fish. They were moving swiftly with the current. They glistened as they swam. Seven heads bent over the water to watch them. Esther was the first to speak.

"Quick, Fayge! Run home and fetch a pot," she cried. "Go quietly," she added. "Don't wake Momme."

She pulled off her apron to use as a net. "Go

Without-fish with Fish

43

further down the bank," she called to the others. "Try to catch the fish in your hands."

Six pairs of hands cupped themselves in the water. The wee fish slid through their fingers. But even the most slippery fish aren't a match for six pairs of hands, not to speak of a net made out of an apron.

"I have two fish," called Reizel. "Quick, the pot!"

"I have four," said Goldie.

"I have one, too," said Kezele.

Into the pot went more and more of the wee fishes. The bottom was covered with them. They squirmed and glistened.

"Teppele," Esther said, "tonight we'll have without-fish *with* fish for supper."

Without-fish *with* fish!

Teppele, Tseppele, Kezele danced with excitement. Kezele's shirttail came out, but no one remembered to tuck it back.

"Let's not tell Momme 'til the fish is cooked," said Reizel. "It will be a surprise."

Esther wasn't sure about the surprise. "Do you know how quiet you would have to be?" she asked.

"We'll be quiet as a mouse," said Teppele.

"Quiet—quiet as a fish," said Tseppele.

What could Esther say after that? One couldn't be quieter than a fish. A fish makes no sound at all. They picked up the pot and set out for home.

Esther tied the kid to a rope outside the house before they went in.

Catching slippery fish with hands and an apron was hard enough. Surprising Momme was even harder. Seven pair of feet had to remember to walk on tiptoe. Seven excited voices had to quiet down to whispers.

First Reizel tiptoed to the bedroom door to see whether Momme was still asleep. She was. Then everyone set to work. Tseppele and Teppele went out into the garden to pull up onions and potatoes. The tiny new potatoes came up clinging to the roots, earth still on them. Fayge washed and scraped them. Kezele brought turf, and Esther built a fire under the tripod. Goldie and Reizel cleaned the tiny fish.

"Sh! Sh!" Each one reminded the others. There was one minute when the surprise was almost spoiled. It was when Kezele stumbled over a stool. He opened his mouth to wail, but Reizel clapped her hands over it just in time. Teppele peeked into the bedroom to see if Momme had awakened. Her eyes seemed open. But when Teppele looked again, they were closed.

The water in the pot was bubbling. Esther dropped in the tiny new potatoes, the young onions, the wee fish. Teppele sniffed happily. A heavenly odor was rising from the pot. At that moment the door opened and Father came in. Reizel put her finger to her lips and led him to the pot. How surprised he was when Esther spooned up the tiny fish.

But the most surprised one was Momme when the family crowded around her bed and set the bowl of fish beside her. It took her a whole minute to realize that this was without-fish *with* fish. They had to tell her over and over how they had caught the fish with Esther's apron and their hands.

"Didn't you hear us, Momme? Didn't you guess?" they asked her.

"We—ll! I guessed you were cooking something," Momme said, "but I didn't dream it would be without-fish *with* fish."

She turned to Dovidel in his cradle.

"You see, Dovidel," she said, "the kind of family you have been born into."

Then she dipped her spoon into the steaming dish.

Father and the children watched until Momme had eaten the last delicious bite. Then they, too, washed

47

their hands, said a blessing, and ate. They ate until the last tiny fish had disappeared, bones and all.

"Good," Teppele said ecstatically, rubbing her stomach.

A faint meh-h-h echoed her.

"It's Gadya," Reizel cried. "He's been tied outside all this time."

She was out of her seat and through the door in a minute.

"Gadya," she asked, as she stooped to untie the little kid, "did *you* make this happen?

"Meh-h-h," Gadya answered.

Did it mean yes or no?

Concerning Momme and Father

BY DAY THE SLEEPING benches were used as seats. At night they became beds. Esther, Fayge, and Goldie slept in one; Reizel, Teppele, and Tseppele in another. Kezele had a sleeping bench to himself. Plump feather beds made the boards soft and comfortable.

Momme had brought the feather beds with her when she came to Father as a bride. Every house had its pile of bedding; pillows, feather beds, sacks of goose-down for new pillows. Year by year the pile grew higher. When the time came for a daughter to marry, the pillows and feather beds were ready for her. It troubled Momme that their own pile was so low. With six daughters, it should have reached the ceiling.

There was much more that Momme had brought with her as a bride. The corner chest was full of homespun linens, tablecloths, sheets, pillowcases, each with Momme's initials embroidered in the center. The children were always admiring the beautiful red letters.

Even lovelier than the embroidered letters was

Momme's crocheted tablecloth, made of rows and rows of wheels, light and delicate. "Like snowflakes," Fayge said.

Most beautiful of all was the beaded wall basket. It was flat on one side, with pockets on the other, all of it covered with flowers made of beads—blue forget-me-nots, pink roses with green stems and curling leaves.

"How did you do it, Momme? Look at those tiny buds!" The children marveled and exclaimed.

All these things Momme had made before she married Father, when she lived in the big house on the square and ate white bread and sugar even on weekdays.

Father was a young student at the time. He had

come from his village to study under their rabbi. At home, he had learned the whole Bible and much besides. He knew the *Torah,* the Five Books of Moses, almost by heart. Now he wanted to master the *Talmud,* great volumes filled with the teachings of the ancient rabbis.

All day and far into the night, he stood before a reading stand in the House of Study. His bed was a bench in the synagogue. He ate what was called "days," his Monday meals with one family, his Tuesday meals with another, a different family for each day. People considered it a good deed to have a student at their table. On Sabbaths, he was a guest at Momme's father's house. Her mother had died the year before. It was in this way that Father and Momme met.

Father—who was not yet Father, but only Avrom Itsik—thought that no one was so lovely as Reb Dovid's motherless daughter with her gentle manners and her quiet eyes.

"She is like the flowers she embroiders, a rose of Sharon!" he thought, glancing at her across the table.

"He is so thin. Perhaps he doesn't get enough to eat on weekdays. I should like to feed him properly," Gittel thought, lowering her eyes. She had never met anyone quite like this laughing, blue-eyed *Talmud* student.

After they were married, they lived on in Grandfather's home so that Father might continue studying.

51

Esther and Fayge were born there. Then Grandfather died and they opened a dry-goods store. It was mostly Momme who looked after the store. Father was too impatient to bargain with housewives and peasant women. By the time that Reizel was born, Father had decided to become a manufacturer. He and a friend would open a shop off the square and manufacture candles.

"Why candles?" Momme asked.

"Why not candles?" said Father.

He grew poetic. "Candles bring light. Candles usher in the Sabbath. Besides, everybody needs them."

It was true. Everybody needed candles. But they did not seem to need precisely the candles that Avrom Itsik made. The store had to be given up to raise money for the candle shop.

Father was sure that all would go well.

"Our luck will be as golden as your curls," he would say to three-year-old Goldie, lifting her high in the air.

But after a year he felt less sure.

One evening he said to Momme, "Gittel, my luck is like Ibn Ezra's."

"Who was Ibn Ezra?" Momme asked.

"One of the Spanish Hebrew poets," Father explained. "A great poet—but without luck! Once he said, 'If I manufactured coffins, nobody would die.'"

Father paused.

"Gittel, if I keep on making candles, women will stop kindling Sabbath lights."

Momme knew what was coming. Father gave up what remained of the candle business, and the family moved to the small house on the lane.

After this Father earned a living in whatever way he could, usually by buying hides and feed from peasants to sell to merchants in town. All week he was away from home, but on Friday he returned. The moment Father walked through the door, the house came to life. He tossed the week's earnings into Momme's lap. He chucked Dovidel under the chin, lifted Kezele in the air. He bent down and pretended he could not get his arms around Teppele and Tseppele. The children laughed and chattered. Momme forgot her worries.

Other families had roast fowl for the Sabbath, fur-lined jackets in winter, new shoes every Passover. *They* had Father.

Fayge's Tree

SEVEN WEEKS AFTER PASSOVER came the festival of *Shevuos. Shevuos* celebrated the giving of the Ten Commandments on Mount Sinai. Except for *Sukkos,* which came in the fall, it was Fayge's favorite holiday.

One of Hannah Rachel's stories was about a princess who had been banished from her father's kingdom and made to work as a kitchen maid. One day in the week she was permitted to wash away the soot and put on her beautiful garments. Then everyone saw that she was a princess.

It seemed to Fayge that on *Shevuos* their house was like that princess. Suddenly, it was beautiful and fragrant with leafy branches and rushes and sweet grasses brought in from the meadow and woods. The "greens" hung from the rafters; they filled the windows; they rustled underfoot—a reminder of the days when the Jewish people harvested their own fields in the Land of Israel.

On this *Shevuos* something besides the greens brought sudden beauty to the little house, something that hung on the east wall, so lovely that even the

55

rebbitzin, the wife of the rabbi, had come to see it. Fayge's own hands had made it. Be patient and you will soon hear what it was.

Fayge had always been different from the rest of the children. There was the day the peasant women came into town, their aprons filled with blueberries. The children popped the berries into their mouths as fast as they could get them. But not Fayge! Fayge kept looking at them.

"They are pretty," she said. "See! They have veils over them, like a bride."

"Silly!" The children laughed. "Berries are to eat, not to look at."

In the synagogue it was all Momme could do to keep the children from running up and down the stairs and around the women's gallery. But Fayge? Fayge sat quietly beside her mother with her head pressed against the railing, looking down through an opening in the curtain. She wasn't praying like Esther. She was looking, just looking. At what? At the *bimah,* the platform where the *Torah* scrolls were read, its wooden railing and canopy carved with pears and apples and curling leaves. Fayge wished that she could go down and curve her hands around a pear.

"Golden hands," Momme called them. They could hem a shirt with stitches so even and tiny one could scarcely see them. They could take scissors and a bit of colored paper; a few snips and the paper became a flower, a bird, a tree. They could plant a real tree,

a tiny one, in the lane where no trees grew and make
it take root and leaf.

It was early in the spring when Fayge planted her
tree. Momme had sent her to the weaver's with the
skeins of linen they had spun during the long winter.
Stepan Weaver lived in a thatched hut, so low that
Fayge could touch the roof with her hand. It was dark
and crowded inside. The loom took up the greater
part of the room. But outside grew a tall tree with
a smooth gray trunk and spreading boughs. Near the
tall tree was the little tree.

Fayge loved the little tree the minute she saw it:
the branches that bent modestly, then turned up at
the tips as if they had to look at heaven; the thin
pointed buds, the color of Momme's copper pots. She
touched the tip of a bud with her finger. She ran her
hand across the smooth silver trunk.

It was then that the unbelievable thing happened.

"You like the tree?" asked the weaver's wife. She
had been watching Fayge. "Dig it up and take it
home. I'll help you."

As in a dream, Fayge dug up the little tree and
carried it back to the muddy lane.

Father laughed when he saw her kneeling on the
ground, pressing the soil around the roots.

"Little foolish one," he said, "what are you doing?
Providing a meal for the goats? They will enjoy the
juicy leaves."

"But, Father," Fayge insisted, "there are goats on

Stepan Weaver's street, and they don't chew up the trees."

"Maybe the goats have respect for Stepan," Father answered, "or for Stepan's dogs."

"Let her be, Avrom." Momme came to Fayge's help. "Maybe the goats will have respect for Fayge, too."

The goats—the little kid as well—did have respect for Fayge, or for the wooden stakes Father drove into the ground as a protecting fence. Fayge watered her tree carefully, making many trips to the lake. The buds opened. Green leaves appeared, folded like tiny green accordions. The leaves drooped in tassels, then opened wide—fluttering green banners.

It was then that the billy goat appeared. The billy goat had respect for no one, neither people, nor trees, nor stakes. All Fayge's time was spent in guarding her tree. When she had to go to school, Kezele or Reizel kept watch for her.

But a day came when Fayge returned from school to find Momme and the children standing forlornly in front of the house. The tree! What had happened to her tree? Fayge flew down the lane. The tree was there, but its straight, slender trunk was snapped in two. Its branches lay drooping on the ground.

"It was the billy goat," Reizel explained. "I couldn't stop him, Fayge. He came right at it with his head down—through the fence and all."

"Like this." Kezele bent his head and ran forward to show her how a billy goat butts.

"Enough! Be quiet!" Momme slapped Kezele's cheek, then patted it as if to say, "I'm sorry, I didn't mean to do that."

"Maybe we can get you another tree," she said to Fayge.

Fayge rushed into the house.

Night came, and the children lay asleep—all but Esther. Esther stirred restlessly. She could hear Father and Momme talking together.

"Fayge has cried herself to sleep," Momme was saying.

"Over a tree?" Father's voice was troubled, impatient. "Fayge needs to have some sense put into her."

Then Momme again. "What Fayge needs is to make something beautiful with those hands of hers. If only we could buy her embroidery thread or beads."

Now Esther could hear Father murmuring his night prayers. Then there was silence. Esther leaned on her elbow, trying to see through the darkness. Momme had lit a small candle and was sitting near the corner chest, snipping at something with her scissors. *It looked like the beaded basket, Momme's beautiful basket with the roses and forget-me-nots.*

"But it can't be," Esther thought. "I mustn't begin imagining things."

She lay back as Momme turned. In a little while she was asleep.

When Esther woke again, it was morning. Momme was crumbling black bread into milk for bread soup. The children were tumbling out of bed, Gadya pulling at the bedclothes. Yesterday, last night, seemed a dream.

Father returned from morning prayers and the family had breakfast. Then quietly, as if it were of no importance, Momme handed something to Fayge.

"Here, Fayge, are some beads I found. Maybe you'd like to make something out of them."

Fayge looked wonderingly at the bowl of colored beads.

61

"Where did you get them, Momme?"

"I had them—in the chest."

"Then it *was* Momme's basket. I didn't imagine it," Esther thought in distress. She wanted to cry out, "Don't take the beads, Fayge. Momme ripped them from her basket. I saw her." But speaking would not put the beads back.

The children had gathered around Fayge and were fingering the beads admiringly.

"Do you know what you could make, Fayge?" said Father. "A *mizrach!*" His quick smile had returned. "I have just the verse for you: 'The *Torah* is a tree of life to them that take hold of it.'"

"What's a *mizrach?*" asked Kezele.

"It's what you hang on the east wall—like in Reb Hayim's house," Esther explained, "so you know which way to turn for prayers. East is where Jerusalem is."

"I never saw a *mizrach* made of beads," Reizel objected.

"You'll see one now," said Father. "Come, Fayge. I'll outline the letters for you."

Carefully and lovingly, Fayge began to make her *mizrach* out of beads. Around the border ran pears and apples with stems and curving leaves like the carved ones in the synagogue, only these glowed red and green and yellow. In the center was the tree. Not the broken tree with branches trailing on the ground, but the living tree! Its silver trunk rose straight and slender. Its branches bowed modestly toward the earth, then turned up at the tips to look toward heaven. Round the tree in beaded Hebrew letters were the words,

> *It is a tree of life to them that grasp it.*
> *Happy is everyone that holdeth it fast.*

Fayge had her tree again.

On the day before *Shevuos,* Father hung the *mizrach* on the eastern wall. Esther framed it with fragrant grasses.

All through the festival neighbors came in to look at Fayge's handiwork. They stood in awe before the *mizrach,* admiring the glowing border, the perfect tree, spelling out the sacred letters.

"The child has your hands, Gittel," they said.

It was a wonder, a marvel.

Only Reizel noticed that another wonder was going on. Gadya, whose stomach, like Teppele's, was never full; who chewed on everything, even Father's shoe if he could get at it, whose favorite food was sweet meadow grass—Gadya had not touched a blade of the grasses that framed Fayge's *mizrach.* He had not even tried to reach them. Twice Reizel found him standing quietly, facing east, his head lifted up, his eyes on the verse.

"He *knows* it's a *mizrach,*" Reizel decided joyfully.

She needed no further proof. Gadya *was* Elijah's kid.

63

Goldie Becomes a Heroine

"THE KID WILL BE as spoiled as Kezele," Momme scolded. "Seven children fussing over it and lugging it around!"

She should have said *six* children. Goldie never picked up the kid. She edged away if it so much as sniffed at her dress.

"If you must fuss, do it out of doors," said Momme.

She opened the door and shooed Gadya out. The children followed.

"Let's go to the meadow," Reizel said. "The strawberries are ripe."

The children loved the tiny strawberries that grew wild in the meadow where Purik, the gooseboy, tended his flocks.

Only Goldie held back.

"Goldie's afraid she'll meet Purik's geese," Reizel said scornfully. "She's just a scared rabbit."

It was true.

Goldie was afraid of everything. She never took the short cut across the pasture for fear of the cows. She kept away from Stepan Weaver's street because of the dogs. She wouldn't go berry-picking for fear of Purik's geese. The very sound of his hissing gander made her scream and run.

"It's a wonder Goldie isn't afraid of the goats," people said. They didn't know that Goldie *was* afraid of goats, even of Gadya. But there were goats everywhere. One had to pass them to go anywhere at all.

Goldie, sitting alone on the doorstep, wished so hard that she were brave. What was the use of being the prettiest of the sisters with curls the color of flax when no one wanted to play with her?

She was glad when Momme called her.

"Go over to Marusha's," Momme said. "Ask her if she can help with the wash next week."

Marusha Litvak had worked in Grandmother's house when Momme was a little girl. One would think that Momme was her own child the way she looked after her. Every time a baby was born, every time Momme had to do something hard like the summer washing, Marusha came over to help her. She didn't even want to be paid.

Goldie flew on her errand. There was nothing she liked better than the early summer washing when all Momme's lovely linens were bleached in the hot sun. Even the crocheted tablecloth was brought out, Momme's beautiful cloth with the lacy wheels. No one, not even Fayge, admired the cloth as much as Goldie did. It made her think of golden-haired princesses, and palaces, and feasts served on golden dishes.

65

Early Tuesday morning Marusha came over and the washing began. Marusha's broad strong hands were as good as a washboard. Soon the clothes were boiling in the steaming copper caldron.

Then down the lane to the lake went Momme and Marusha, carrying the baskets of wet clothes. The children followed, this time trying *not* to splash in the mud puddles. Esther carried Dovidel. Reizel wanted to take Gadya along, but Momme said, "And have him track mud over the clean clothes?" So the little kid was left at home.

At the lake the washing began all over again. Marusha doused each piece in the water, then pounded it with a big wooden stick.

"Ho!" No dirt could hide in a sheet with Marusha pounding it. Esther and Fayge rinsed each piece in the lake. Reizel and Goldie spread them on the grass to dry.

The sun beat down, which was just what Momme wanted. As soon as a piece was dry, she sprinkled it again. Sprinkle, dry, sprinkle, dry, all through the day. There was nothing like sunshine to bleach clothes snowy white.

The sun set at last. But the washing was not over. Bleaching the linens took three days, not one.

On the third day, Momme brought out the crocheted cloth. Carefully she spread it in the sun to bleach.

All the children gathered about the cloth, admiring it.

"May I touch it to see if it's dry? May I sprinkle it?" Goldie kept asking.

Noon came. It was time to go home for dinner. "Someone has to stay here to watch the cloth," Momme said.

"I will! Let me," each one shouted.

How happy Goldie was when Momme chose *her!*

"Take good care of the cloth," Momme warned her as she went off. "Don't take your eyes off it for a minute."

Goldie was left alone with the precious cloth. Bees buzzed drowsily. The air smelled of clean wash and clover and warm sunshine. Goldie hummed a little song of happiness. All the while her eyes were on the lacy cloth. She kept her eyes on it so steadily that the wheels seemed to be going round. Goldie's thoughts began going around with the wheels.

"When I grow up," she thought, "I will live in a grand big house with floors like wax and wear silk dresses like Aunt Sophie." Aunt Sophie was Father's beautiful sister who had married a rich merchant and gone to live in far Russia. "I'll even scrub the floors in silk dresses. Every day I'll spread a cloth on the table, a beautiful cloth with three hundred and eight wheels like Momme's."

Goldie was so busy daydreaming, she failed to notice something white moving in the distance. It was Purik's flock of geese coming across the meadow. The gander ran ahead.

Hs—s—s—s—!

Goldie looked up quickly. The gander was coming toward her—across the meadow, down the lane, through the mud puddles. His neck was stretched forward. His wicked eyes were red. He hissed as he ran. The flock of geese followed, their wings outspread.

Goldie screamed and jumped up from the grass to run. Then her eyes fell on Momme's cloth.

"Purik! Purik!" she called to the gooseboy. There was no answer. "He's probably hiding somewhere laughing at me," Goldie thought. She looked despairingly from the geese to the cloth, from the cloth to the geese. Then she ran—not *away* from the gander, but *toward* him. The wooden beater was lying on the ground. She picked it up as she ran.

The gander's bill was almost in her face. "Go away," Goldie screamed, waving the big stick. "Don't you dare track mud over Momme's cloth."

She looked straight into the gander's wicked eyes. The gander hissed, drew in his neck and turned. All the geese turned after him.

"Hurrah for Goldie! Hurrah for Goldie!" It was Reizel and her friend Dena who were shouting. They had come down the lane in time to see Goldie drive off the geese.

"Goldie saved Momme's cloth. You should have

seen Goldie drive off the gander!" The story went from one mouth to another. Goldie had become a heroine. Everyone wanted to play with her now.

But what Goldie could not understand was why she had suddenly stopped being afraid. She wasn't afraid, now, of cows, of dogs, of geese, of goats, of anything. When Gadya came poking at her with his pink nose, she lifted him right up in her arms.

At Frume Leah's

AFTER WASHDAY came ironing day. The linens weren't ironed at home. They weren't ironed by heat. They were pressed smooth in Frume Leah's heavy mangle.

Frume Leah had been Momme's mother's friend. She lived in a solidly built house with a center hall and four large rooms. It stood in a big yard with sheds and barns and goose pens. You always smelled something good when you went up the three steps into Frume Leah's house, fresh bread coming out of the oven, geese roasting, onions frying in goose fat. This was because Reb Nisan, Frume Leah's husband, had a contract with the army. Twice every week they baked great round loaves of black bread for the companies of soldiers who guarded the border. Once each week they sent roast geese to the barracks, geese that had browned slowly in long earthen dishes, twenty at a time.

It was to Frume Leah's house the family went on ironing day.

73

Again Marusha came to help. She led the way, carrying the heaviest basket of clean clothes. Esther and Fayge carried the two others. Momme carried Dovidel. Reizel carried Gadya—to keep him from muddying his feet. The rest followed. Through the yard they went, past the pens where Frume Leah fattened the geese, past a great pile of split logs. Kezele had to throw back his head to see the top. Beyond the woodpile was the open shed where Frume Leah kept the mangle.

It was a very large mangle. A wide wooden roller and a heavy board with a handle were set into a frame. Fastened to the top of the board was a box full of heavy stones.

Esther took the baby from Momme, and the work began.

A sheet, folded over and dampened, was wound smoothly around the roller, and the roller inserted under the board. Marusha grasped the handle and pushed hard. The board moved slowly forward, down! Again, forward, down! Grooves, cut into the underside of the board, set the roller turning. The box of stones weighed it down. Something else added weight. Kezele and Gadya were riding on the box.

"*V'yoh!*" Kezele shouted as if he were driving a horse. "*V'yoh!*"

The sheet came off the roller, soft and smooth as silk.

"Come down, Kezele. It's Teppele's turn," Reizel called to him.

Reizel was too big for rides, but she could supervise the others. Kezele scrambled down reluctantly, and Teppele climbed up. Gadya stayed on.

A second sheet was wound around the roller, and Marusha started again. Push, forward, down! Push, forward, down! Sweat stood out on her forehead.

"It's too hard for one person. Let me help," Momme said. Her hands were already on the handle beside Marusha's. Marusha removed Momme's hands as if she were a little child. "No," she said firmly, "this is not for you."

"She is right, Gittel." Frume Leah had come out and was calling from the top step. "This is no work to be doing so soon after childbirth. I'll send Natasha out to help. She is strong as an ox."

Her eyes fell on Teppele, perched on the box of stones.

"I remember," she said to Momme, "when you and my Mirel, peace to her, used to ride on that box."

She turned abruptly and went back into the house. Natasha, the servant woman, came out. Her sleeves were rolled up, showing bulging muscles. She and Marusha grasped the handle together. The board moved easily across the roller.

Momme's thoughts turned to her childhood. How many rides she and Mirel had taken on that box of stones. Everyone who used Reb Nisan's mangle offered rides to his little daughter and her friend. Now Mirel, peace to her, was in the "true world." She had died suddenly, when still a young girl, from some sort of sickness in the throat. And she, Gittel, was the mother of eight children.

The laughter of the little ones, the bleating of Gadya, the gabbling of the geese came to Momme as if from far away. She was a child again in her mother's home. On the holiday table was a goose— not just the *draybe,* the neck, gizzard, and feet, such as she divided among her own children. This was a whole goose, plump with stuffing, its skin crisped brown.

Thoughts of the goose led to thoughts of goose feathers. Her mother had begun saving them from the time that she was born. There must be pillows and feather beds for her little daughter to carry with her when she grew up and had a home of her own. Where, Momme wondered, were the feathers for her own little daughters to come from? The only goose one saw on their table from one year to the next was the one that provided their Passover fat.

An excited gabbling from the goose pen brought Momme back to the present. Gadya had climbed to the top of the woodpile and come down the farther side by leaps, landing in the pen. The frightened geese were milling about frantically, the children screaming. Reizel climbed over the fence and grabbed Gadya in her arms. She was climbing back with him when Frume Leah came out to see what the excitement was about.

Reizel hurried over to her, the little kid still in her arms.

"Gadya didn't mean to frighten the geese," she explained earnestly. "He just wanted to play with them. He's a very friendly kid. See, he wants to make friends with *you*."

She looked anxiously at the little kid, who had begun licking Frume Leah's hand.

"Is that the kid who came to your table on *seder* night?" Frume Leah asked.

Reizel nodded.

"Elijah brought him. His name is Gadya."

"It's a pity Elijah didn't leave one of his sisters," Frume Leah said, all her smile wrinkles showing. "A milk goat would be useful."

77

"That's what Father said," Reizel told her. "But, Frume Leah, Gadya is useful too—and so clever. Do you know what he does when our baby cries? He butts the cradle to make it rock—and . . . and . . ." Reizel searched in her mind for some further example of Gadya's usefulness, and found one. "He saves us from the sin of waste. We don't waste anything any more. Gadya eats the potato peelings and carrot tops and spoiled cabbage leaves—even onion skins."

She was sure that this would impress Frume Leah. Wasn't Momme always saying, "It is a sin to waste food. What one recites a blessing over must be treated with respect." Even crumbs had to be gathered up for the chickens or the birds.

Frume Leah *was* impressed. "Maybe you can save *me* from the sin of waste," she said. "I have a whole pot of goose *gribines* that I don't know what to do with."

Teppele, who had edged up to them, felt her mouth water. *Gribines* were the crisp bits of cracklings and onions left over when the fat was rendered.

Frume Leah turned toward the shed where Momme was packing the smooth linens into a basket.

"May I take the young ones in for a little treat, Gittel?" she asked.

Momme nodded her permission, thanking Frume Leah for her kindness.

Up the three steps went the children with Gadya tripping after them. In the big kitchen Frume Leah cut a wedge out of one of the great rounds of black bread, sliced it down, and spread each piece thick with fat cracklings and onions.

Reizel took her first delicious bite. Then she stooped, and patted Gadya lovingly on his two bumps. What a kid Elijah had sent them! Even when he got into mischief, good came of it.

At Frume Leah's

Tseppele Goes on a Journey

TSEPPELE AND FATHER were going on a visit to Grandmother and Grandfather, a whole day's journey into the country. Not by train! Tseppele had never heard of a train. They were going with Telegraph, the wagoner.

Why of all the children had Tseppele been chosen for the journey? Why not Teppele, her twin; or Esther the eldest; or Kezele? Because Tseppele was named after Grandma's mother, Tsippe. "My little mother," Grandma called her. When Father had written that he was coming on a visit, she had answered, "I beg you to give me the joy of seeing my *mommele*, Tsippe."

All the family including Gadya were in the square to see them off.

Gadya nuzzled Tseppele affectionately. Then he gave her a comical push toward the wagon. Then he nuzzled her again.

"Make up your mind, Gadya," said Father, laughing. "Do you want her to go? Then why so much affection? Do you want her to stay? Then why do you hurry her away?"

He lifted Tseppele into the wagon and tucked her in among the bundles. Then he climbed in himself.

"V'yoh!" Telegraph shouted to his horse. A flick of the whip, a pull on the reins, and they were off.

"Have a good trip, Tseppele! Have a good trip!"

The children called and waved until the wagon was out of sight.

How empty the house seemed when the children returned home! Who would have thought that Tseppele would be so missed, plain, plump, slow-moving Tseppele, with thin braids begging to be pulled!

"What do you suppose Tseppele is doing now?" Teppele asked as Momme stirred the oatmeal gruel for their dinner.

"Probably walking," Momme answered.

"Walking? Not riding?" The children looked up in astonishment.

"If they have come to a hill she is walking," said Momme. "Telegraph's horse has enough to do to carry his old bones up a hill without carrying the passengers. I shouldn't be surprised if your father were behind the wagon pushing."

"But Momme," Reizel asked, "if Telegraph is so slow, why is he called Telegraph?"

"For the same reason a fool is called Wiseman," said Momme.

Night came. Momme opened the sleeping benches

and lay the feather beds across them, wondering as always how she could get more feathers. Tseppele had gone on a journey. Within a week, with God's help, she would return. But a time would come when Momme's young daughters would go off, not to their grandparents' home—to their husbands' homes. It would be her glad duty as a mother to provide them with bedding. But where were the feathers to come from?

The children, snuggling down in their beds, did not know what Momme was thinking. *Their* thoughts were still of Tseppele. Reizel and Teppele had thought it would be fun to have a bed to themselves. Now Teppele would gladly have squeezed over to the very edge to have Tseppele between them.

"What is Tseppele doing now?"

The question kept coming up all through the week until Momme said, "Enough! When Tseppele comes home you will ask her and you will know."

The day came at last. Soon, soon Tseppele would be with them, Tseppele who had been to far places and seen who knows what wonderful sights. All the family waited for her in the square.

"*V'yoh!*" Telegraph's wagon clattered over the cobblestones.

There was Father lifting Tseppele from the cart.

Her cheeks were a little rosier, her eyes sleepier. Otherwise she looked exactly the same, plain, plump, her thin braids dancing.

"Tseppele, Tseppele!"

83

Gadya jumped on her in welcome. Teppele hugged her. They all hugged her. They plied her with questions. "Tell us—" "Where were you—" "What's in the bundle?" "How—?"

"Let her be," said Momme. "She has just come more than a day's journey—all night in the wagon—and you are already at her with your questions."

And Momme marched Tseppele ahead of them to the house.

"Here, Tseppele, eat," she said, setting a bowl of hot oatmeal porridge in Tseppele's lap.

The children had to wait until Tseppele's wooden spoon scraped the bottom of the bowl. Then out came the questions.

"Tell us about it, Tseppele—from the beginning."

Tseppele tried. "I rode in the wagon," she said. "Then I fell asleep, and when I woke up I was at Grandpa's house. The aunts took off my shoes."

"The aunts! Are they pretty?"

"Very pretty," said Tseppele.

"In what way pretty?" Goldie begged her.

Tseppele considered the matter.

"Their cheeks are red—like the poppies."

"Are there poppies at Grandpa's place?" asked Fayge.

"Poppies, of course," said Tseppele, "with pods. I ate the seeds in the sack."

"The seeds were in a sack?"

"No. The seeds were in my pocket. *I* was in the sack."

The children looked at Tseppele in astonishment.
"You were in a sack?"

"When we went to dig potatoes," Tseppele explained. "The rain came down—hard. So Aunt Beila said, 'We mustn't let Tseppele get wet,' and they lowered the potato sack over me and held it. And I ate the poppy seeds."

Tseppele threw back her head and crooked her fingers to show how one empties a pod of poppy seeds into one's mouth.

Fayge's thoughts flew to the poppy-bordered field. She could see the brown potato field and the nodding red poppies. She could see the aunts with cheeks like poppies holding the sack over Tseppele, while the rain came down and the sun shone through the rain.

But Teppele was thinking of the poppy seeds.

"Greedy! Why did you eat up all the poppy seeds? You could have saved a few pods for us."

"I did," Tseppele said, "but when the train came in I was so frightened, I dropped them."

"Train?" This was a new word. "What is that—a train?"

Tseppele tried to explain. "A—a kind of wagon,

hitched to another wagon, and another wagon, and another wagon. But closed—and no horse."

"They unhitched the horse?"

"No!" said Tseppele. "It goes without a horse!"

"It goes without a horse?" The children were sure that Tseppele must be joking.

"Without a horse," Tseppele insisted. "And fire and smoke came out—and NOISE." Tseppele clapped her hands over her ears to show how terrible the noise was. "So I cried and dropped the poppy seeds, but Aunt Sophie—"

"Aunt Sophie!"

Even the train was forgotten!

Tseppele had seen Aunt Sophie, who lived in far Russia in a house that had a balcony with flowers, and floors as slippery as glass. No sand on them at all! Momme had told them about it often. Aunt Sophie who wore a silk dress and a hat!

"You saw Aunt Sophie! No!"

"Yes," said Tseppele. "She came to visit Grandma, so Uncle Eli took me to the train. Aunt Sophie came out of it. And she said, 'Don't cry, Tseppele,' and gave me the doll with the hat."

"A doll with a hat!"

This was *too* much. This the children could not believe.

"No!" they said in chorus.

"Yes," said Tseppele.

She reached into the bundle beside her and drew out a doll! Not a rag doll! A wax doll, with blue

eyes, with cheeks like poppies, with a hat on, a hat with a feather.

And that was how a doll in a silk dress and real hat came to live in the little house with the white-washed walls and sand-sprinkled floor. Momme set her on the shelf, where she sat demurely beside the Sabbath candlesticks.

News of the doll spread quickly. Not a girl in town was lucky enough to have a hat. And here was a little doll that had one. Children stopped Tseppele as she passed. They questioned her:

"Do you really have a doll with a hat, Tseppele?"

"Will you let us see it, Tseppele?"

"May we touch it, Tseppele?"

They appealed to Tseppele in their arguments.

"The hitched-together wagons did so run without a horse, didn't they, Tseppele?"

"Show us how big the noise was, Tseppele."

Now it was Teppele who followed Tseppele around.

"All the time they ask me. All the time, I have to tell them," said Tseppele.

Her shoulders went up, her hands went out, her thin braids danced importantly.

Kezele's Great Adventure

"TEPPELE, NOT ONE—Goldie, not two—Fayge, not three—Tseppele, not four—"

Reizel was counting to see how many of the children had had their wishes come true since the coming of Gadya. Counting people was unlucky. But if you said "*not* one, *not* two" it was all right.

"Who will be the next one?" Reizel wondered.

The next was little brother, Kezele. Kezele's adventure began with a silver pointer kept high up on a cupboard shelf. The pointer belonged to Momme, and was more precious to her than any of the treasures in the chest. It was called a *yad,* which means hand, because its tip was shaped like a tiny hand with a pointing finger.

Long before any of the children were born, when Momme herself was a little girl, the *yad* had pointed to the letters in a *Sefer Torah,* a great scroll in which the Five Books of Moses were written down. Wherever men met to pray, the Bible lesson of the week was read out of a *Torah* scroll.

Such a scroll, covered with a beautiful velvet

mantle, stood in a special ark in a room in Momme's grandfather's house. There neighbors gathered for their weekday prayers. Every Monday and Thursday, the scroll was taken from the ark and unrolled. Then Grandfather read the lesson for the week, pointing to each word with the silver *yad*. Momme—she was called little Gittel in those days—stood on tiptoe to watch. The tiny hand with its pointing finger fascinated her.

Long after, when she was grown up and married, and had moved out of the big house, Momme kept the *Torah* pointer as a remembrance of her grandfather. She would not part with it, not even in the hard year when they sold their *Hanukah* lamp.

"Of what use is a *Torah* pointer without a *Sefer Torah?*" Father asked.

Momme did not answer. She herself did not know why she clung to the silver *yad*—until Kezele was born. Her first son! They named him after Momme's grandfather. The house was filled with friends and relatives on the day of his circumcision. From her bed in the inner room Momme could hear the voice of Reb Hayim, "This little one, may he grow big." Then blessings and good wishes. "*Mazeltov!* Good luck! May you raise your son to the *Torah,* to the wedding canopy, and to good deeds."

Momme watched as the midwife laid her little son on her bed to wrap him in his swaddling clothes. One hand was curled up under his chin. A tiny finger, like the finger of the *yad,* rested on his cheek. In that moment Momme knew that it was for her son she had kept the *Torah* pointer all these years. He would grow up a good and learned man, the head of a household. A day would come when he would engage a scribe to write a new *Sefer Torah.* There could not be too many copies of the Holy Law. Joyfully, he would adorn the scroll with the silver *yad.* She could see it gleaming against the velvet *Torah* mantle, its tiny finger ready to point once more to the sacred letters.

Four years had passed since that day. Now it was Kezele who was fascinated by the tiny hand. Momme had placed it on the topmost cupboard shelf to keep it out of his reach. There it lay on the day of the great adventure. But before you hear about the adventure, you must meet *Todros the Gentle Giant.*

Todros, the town porter, lived with his widowed mother in a thatched hut near the lake. Six foot four he stood, strong as an ox, quick with his fist, though gentle when not angered; but not exactly quick of wit.

To Kezele, he was a Samson-the-strong, a hero. With good reason! It was Todros who carried him to safety on the spring day the rushing waters of the stream carried their bridge away. Kezele and the twins should not have crossed the bridge without permission from Momme. Now they stood on the far bank looking forlornly at the rushing waters. How could they get home? Kezele began to wail. In that moment, Todros came striding down the path, a heavy pack on his shoulders.

"Don't cry, Kezele," he said, setting down his pack.

Before Kezele knew what was happening, Todros had lifted him high on his shoulders and was wading through the swirling waters. On the home side of the stream Todros set him down, safe and dry. Then he waded back for Teppele and Tseppele.

From that day Todros was Kezele's hero. People smiled when they saw the two together, Kezele three foot three and Todros six foot four.

"A perfect match," they would say. "Kezele has the brains and Todros the brawn." Then they would laugh as if what they had said was very clever.

It troubled Kezele that people—even Father—laughed at Todros. Did someone's roof leak? Father would say, "Todros must have stood up in your home. You might have known his head would knock a hole in the ceiling." Did a *matza* come out too thick to use? Father called it a "Todros *matza*."

Once Kezele heard Momme say, "Let Todros be! He is a good son to his mother."

"Who said that Todros isn't a good son?" Father countered. "He obeys the law exactly. 'And thy mother shalt thou fear.'"

Then Father told the story about the day Todros

was crossing the lake in a rowboat. Suddenly a storm came up. The waves rose high. The boat rocked.

"Save me! Save me!" Todros cried. "If I drown my mother will kill me."

"Did Todros really say that?" Reizel asked.

"How should I know?" Father answered. "I tell you what I have heard."

Kezele, listening, felt troubled and mixed up inside. He wanted to shout, "Stop, Father! Don't you dare talk that way about Todros!"

But one doesn't shout at one's father.

Kezele threw himself on the floor and began kicking his heels.

"What has gotten into the child?" Father said. "Kezele, get up this minute."

Momme didn't say anything. She lifted Kezele in her arms and carried him into the next room.

Now are you ready to hear what happened during the week of the summer fair?

It began in the early morning.

"Don't leave the house alone. There are gypsies around," Momme cautioned Reizel and Goldie as she left for the market, taking Dovidel with her. She was to help Hannah Rachel, who had boiled a great pot of sweet and sour fish to sell to the peasants. Esther and Fayge were helping at the *bagel* woman's stand.

Peasants from miles around came to town on fair days. They drove in in carts loaded with vegetables and eggs and cackling hens. They came on foot, carrying a single duck, or a hen, or driving a cow or goat. Shopkeepers piled their wares on the cobblestones. Housewives offered homemade food for sale: ginger-stick candies, little round cakes boiled in honey, pickled herring, sweet and sour fish. Bargainers argued and shouted. Wandering beggars squatted in the gutter, singing as they held out their beggar sacks. It was hard to stay home on a fair day.

"We don't both have to watch the house," Reizel decided after Momme had left. "You watch first, Goldie, and I'll watch later." And Reizel was off with her friend Dena. Gadya and the twins trailed after.

Goldie and Kezele sat down on the doorstep. A hen in the road was taking a dust bath. Nothing else stirred. It was so quiet in the lane, the songs of the beggars came to them from the square. Songs always called to Goldie. She knew the melodies for all the festivals. "Sing 'When Israel Went Out of Egypt,' the children would say to her, or "Sing 'Rejoice and Be Glad,'" and Goldie would sing the lilting, joyful songs. But she liked best the pleading chants of the solemn fall festivals. The beggars' songs that came to her from the square made her think of these—sad songs, full of longing. Goldie could not resist them.

"Stay here, Kezele. Don't move from your place.

I'll be back in a few minutes," Goldie said. And she too ran off.

The hen finished its dust bath. Still Goldie had not returned. Kezele wandered into the house. The cupboard door was ajar. On the top shelf lay the *Torah* pointer with its tiny hand. No one was around to say, "Don't, Kezele."

Kezele pushed a bench in front of the cupboard, set a stool on the bench, and climbed up. The stool wobbled, but he paid no heed. His hand had closed over the precious *yad*.

Down Kezele climbed with his treasure. On the doorstep he unwrapped and examined it. The tiny finger pointed downward, begging to be used. Kezele stooped and began tracing pictures in the dust.

"Good morning to you, young one," said a deep, pleasant voice.

Kezele looked up. A dark, handsome stranger with gold rings in his ears had come down a side path. He was leading a horse by a rope. It wasn't a tired, bony horse like Telegraph's. This one was smooth and sleek, and tossed its head with spirit.

Kezele could not take his eyes from the horse. The stranger's eyes were on the silver pointer.

"Is your mother home, little boy?" he asked.

"No," said Kezele. "She's in the market. Goldie will be back soon."

"I'm going to the market myself," said the stranger, smiling. When he smiled his mustache turned up and his white teeth gleamed. "Come, I'll take you to your mother—on my horse. You can take your toy along."

He lifted the delighted Kezele to the horse's back and set off on a run. How proud Kezele felt!

"Momme will be surprised when I ride into the market on this fine horse," he thought.

But the stranger didn't turn into the market. He took the road to the lake. Kezele saw tents and a covered wagon in the meadow.

"You said you would take me to Momme," he protested as the stranger stopped before the wagon and lifted him down.

"So I will. There is no hurry. Here. Let me have that toy of yours. You might lose it." The stranger reached out for the silver pointer.

"It's Momme's *yad*." Kezele held the pointer fast.

"Give it to me, you little devil."

The man was no longer smiling. He stood directly in front of Kezele, a fierce scowl on his face.

Suddenly Kezele remembered Momme's warning, "There are gypsies around." He bent his head and ducked between the stranger's parted legs. Across the meadow Kezele raced, his heart thumping. He could hear the gypsy close behind. Ahead lay the path to the market and safety.

At that moment Kezele's feet caught in the root of a tree. Down he went!

Meh-h-h!

Gadya had appeared out of nowhere, and was coming toward the gypsy like a little fury, his head bent, his new horns ready to butt.

Meh-h-h-h!

The gypsy saw him and turned quickly aside. With one hand, he grabbed hold of Kezele's shirttail. The other was reaching for the silver pointer—when a great hairy fist came down on it.

"Run, Kezele!" said a familiar voice.

Todros had come to his help again.

Without realizing it, Kezele had been running toward Todros' hut. He picked himself up and raced on, the pointer safe in his hand.

From the top of the hill, Kezele looked back, anxious about his friend. Todros and the gypsy were rolling on the ground. Two more gypsies were running toward them. One brandished a big thorn stick. Kezele turned and raced to the market.

"Momme! Father! Esther!" he screamed, making his way past peasant carts, through flocks of gabbling geese and ducks and chickens. Momme heard his cries above all the noises of the market. She took Dovidel in her arms and ran.

A crowd had gathered around Kezele. The gay head shawls of the peasant women touched the sober shawls of the townswomen. The crowd parted to let Momme through. Kezele grabbed her hand and pulled her toward the path.

"Save Todros! They're killing Todros," he cried hysterically.

But when the crowd reached the meadow, it was not Todros, but the gypsies who needed saving. They lay sprawled on the ground, bruised and cowering. Todros, with his back to the lake, towered over them. The thorn stick was in Todros' hand.

The gypsies arose in relief as the crowd drew near.

"That one!" said the leader sullenly, pointing to Todros. "He is a bull, a devil! Did I take the boy's silver?" he demanded. "You see that he has it."

For the first time Momme noticed the *Torah* pointer in Kezele's hand. Bit by bit the story came out, how Kezele had climbed up and taken down the pointer—he only wanted to touch the little finger—how the gypsy had put him on his fine horse and promised him a ride to the market, but brought him to the meadow instead; how he had tried to take away Momme's *yad,* but he, Kezele, had held it tight and ducked between the gypsy's legs.

"He almost got it anyway, when I tripped over the root," Kezele explained, "but Todros came."

Kezele turned admiringly toward his hero. So did everyone around him. Todros was looking with awe at the precious thing that he had saved. His big hairy finger touched the tiny finger gently.

That day everybody in town talked about Todros, not about Todros' *matza,* or the stormy day he took a ride in a boat. They told how singlehanded he had fought three gypsies and saved the *Torah* pointer that was Gittel's inheritance from her grandfather.

"That Todros!" they said. "A Samson. An Og-King-of-Bashan!"

Kezele's eyes glowed with pride in his hero.

"Gadya, it was really *you* who saved Momme's *yad,* wasn't it?" The family had returned home and Reizel was out in the yard talking to the kid. "Now don't say you didn't. Todros told me he heard you bleating. He said that he was in the house getting something to eat and your bleating made him come out. Todros is very brave, but he wouldn't have known about the gypsy if it weren't for you."

Gadya had turned and was looking anxiously toward the house. From within came Kezele's excited voice, still talking about his hero.

"Of course, I won't tell," Reizel assured Gadya. "But it's nice to know."

The Dress with the Golden Coins

"KEZELE, WHAT HAVE you been doing to yourself?" Esther cried.

Kezele had come into the house, his face streaked with sweat and dust. His shirt clung to him.

"Helping Purik chase the geese," Kezele explained. "They got into a garden. Was that a job!" he said importantly. "The geese wouldn't listen even to Purik."

"Of course not," said Goldie. "Why do you suppose people say, 'like threatening geese'? *You* threaten and the geese do as they please. Silly things!"

"But useful," said Momme.

She wasn't thinking of the goose meat, though what is more delicious than roast goose; nor of the 103 goose fat. It was the goose feathers and goose down Momme was thinking of.

"Momme," said Reizel, "do you know whose garden the geese got into? Buna Sasha's, whose mother had the dress with the golden coins. Tell us the story, Momme. You haven't told it in a long time."

"A story!" said Kezele, climbing into Momme's lap. Dovidel was already there, but Momme's lap was broad enough for both children. The sisters gathered close to hear their favorite story.

"Reb Yosef was the richest man in town," Momme began. "He owned the mill and the oil press, and lived in a fine house with an orchard and gardens that reached all the way to the lake. It is the same orchard that now belongs to Reb Sender. Reb Yosef, moreover, was a pious man who supported schools and scholars. When his son reached the proper age for marriage, he sent for Hayim Yudel the matchmaker.

"'Search throughout the land for a fitting wife for my son Yitzhak,' he said. 'She must come of a family steeped in learning. And she herself must be pious and gentle, a maiden in a thousand.'

"The matchmaker set out at once. From town to town he went, from province to province. After many weeks he returned and reported to Reb Yosef.

"'I have found the perfect wife for your son. She

is descended from ten generations of rabbis. And she herself is gentle and modest, a maiden with every virtue. Moreover, it may be said of her as of Rivkah, in the Bible, 'And the damsel was fair to look upon.' Indeed her name is Rivkah. It is a match decreed in heaven.'

"Hayim Yudel paused.

" 'Well?' said Reb Yosef impatiently.

" 'There is a difficulty. She is an orphan and has no dowry.' "

Momme's daughters knew very well what a dowry was. It was the marriage gift a father was expected to provide for his daughters—money, linens, bedding, a fine plush coat.

" 'Was it a dowry I asked for or a fitting wife for

my son?' Reb Yosef demanded. 'Take me to this maiden. If she is as you say, I will shower her with more gifts than Abraham's servant showered on Rivkah.' "

The children nodded approvingly. Yitzhak and Rivkah were the Hebrew names for Isaac and Rebekah. It was exciting to hear of a Yitzhak and Rivkah in their own town like the Isaac and Rebekah of the Bible.

Momme went on, "The end of the matter is that what happened in the Bible happened again. They said to the maiden, 'Will you go with this man?' and she said, 'I will go.' And Yitzhak took Rivkah to be his wife and he loved her.

"As for Reb Yosef, he was so pleased with the bride that he had a dress made for her embroidered with coins of gold. There were so many coins that the dress could stand by itself."

"Now tell us what happened to the golden coins," the children begged, when Momme came to the end of the story. And Momme continued.

"It is written in the *Talmud,* 'If your wife is short, bend down to listen to her advice.' So it was with Yitzhak and Rivkah. Yitzhak was a tall, strapping man, hot-tempered and impatient, and Rivkah was a tiny, gentle woman; but he hung on her words as if each one were a pearl. Two daughters they were blessed with. Then misfortune came. Yitzhak died suddenly as he was lifting a heavy millstone in place.

It happened in the very moment a third daughter was born.

"Neighbors gathered about Rivkah and her new-born daughter. 'Poor infant,' they said, weeping, 'an orphan from her birth. She must be named after her father.' And they suggested girls' names that sounded like Yitzhak: Yiskah, Yittah.

"But Rivkah said, 'Yitzhak means laughter. My Yitzhak's daughter shall be called Fraida (Joy).'

"And Fraida the child was named.

"Reb Yosef's daughter-in-law was indeed a woman of valor. By herself she raised her three daughters and led them to the wedding canopy. She cut the golden coins from her wedding dress to provide them with dowries.

"When the youngest daughter had married and followed her husband to another town, Rivkah said, 'Now my work is done. I will go to die in Jerusalem.' She took the remaining coins and set out for the Holy Land."

"But she didn't die," the sisters chimed in.

"No," said Momme. "It is written, 'The air of the Land of Israel makes one wise.' In Jerusalem, Rivkah married again and raised a second family. One of her sons is an artist, skilled in all manner of handiwork. Out of the stone of Jerusalem he fashioned a cup and engraved on it the holy places: the tomb of our mother Rachel, the wailing wall, the cave of Machpelah. I saw the cup when Fraida brought it to show

107

her sister. With the cup came a note, 'To the learned Zvi Hersch, son of Aharon, from me his brother-in-law in the holy city of Jerusalem, may it be rebuilt speedily in our day.'

"May it be so! Amen," Momme concluded.

Then she added a moral to the story. "The important thing is to grow up good and modest Jewish daughters. Go, Esther! Go, Faygele. Review the Bible portion for the week."

The children did not know that they themselves were to add a new chapter to the story.

A Hero Appears

AT THE HEIGHT of the summer heat came the Three Weeks, a time of mourning for the destruction of the Holy Temple in Jerusalem. The lake sparkled invitingly. It called to the children to splash in, to swim and dive, and to tread water. But bathing was forbidden. Was one to enjoy such pleasures as bathing in the very season when enemies had twice destroyed the Holy Temple?

If someone had said to Momme, "But these things happened thousands of years ago," she would have answered, "All the more reason to mourn. Almost two thousand years have passed and the Temple is still in ruins."

But no one thought of asking. The long, dull days dragged on. A week before *Tisha B'Av,* the fast that concludes the Three Weeks, the children were sitting listlessly on the doorstep, when Reizel's friend Dena came up with an idea.

109

"Let's play 'Follow the Leader.' "

"Again?" said Reizel.

"This will be different," Dena explained. "We'll let Gadya be the leader."

Eyes brightened. The children formed in line. Reizel coaxed Gadya to the front and gave him a little push.

Gadya skipped.

The children skipped.

Gadya raced across the square.

The children raced across the square.

Gadya turned down a dusty lane.

The children turned down the lane.

Gadya rubbed his nose against a stone wall.

The children rubbed their noses against the stone wall.

Gadya jumped to the top of the wall.

Everybody stood still.

They couldn't jump to the top of the wall. It was too high. This was the wall that enclosed Reb Sender's orchard.

"Get Gadya to come down, Reizel," Dena said. "We'll start again."

But Reizel was no longer interested in the game. She was staring at the trees that rose on the other side of the wall. Tempting green pears hung from the branches.

"Let's climb a tree," Reizel said. "We'll throw down pears for everyone."

"How will you get over the wall?" Teppele asked.

"You can boost us up."

"But the pears aren't ripe."

"They'll be good anyway."

A tall sunflower watched as Dena and Reizel clambered to the top of the wall, pushed from behind by Goldie, the twins, Kezele, and his friend Zalman. Once on top, it was easy to slip down into the orchard and climb the nearest tree.

"Hold out your skirts! Catch!" Reizel called down from the crotch where she sat.

A handful of hard pears came tumbling over the wall. The next moment there was a fierce barking.

"Yap, yap! Yaarr-rr!"

The children had forgotten about the watchdogs. There were two of them, red-eyed, shaggy-haired, with long fangs like wolves'. They bounded through the orchard to the foot of the tree and looked up, barking and snarling.

Reizel and Dena clung tightly to the bough. Goldie tried to distract the dogs by throwing stones. Kezele raced home for Esther.

Flushed and out of breath, Esther turned into the lane just as a young stranger entered from the other end. Later, Esther remembered that the stranger was tall, with broad shoulders and friendly eyes. Now he vaulted over the wall. It is hard to say exactly what happened next. Afterward, each one told a different story. Reizel insisted that the stranger pronounced two mysterious words containing the secret letters of the Holy Name. She said that the minute the dogs heard them, they stopped barking and slinked away.

Teppele agreed that the dogs went off, but thought it was to get something which the boy had thrown into the tall grass. "Probably a bone—with meat."

Goldie scoffed at both ideas. "Why," she asked, "would anyone go around carrying a meat bone? The stranger probably knew the dogs. His voice sounded as if he did."

Esther had her own idea, but she kept it to herself. Dogs attacked people who were afraid of them. If one were brave and fearless, he could go near them unharmed. She wanted to thank the young man for coming so bravely to her sister's help. But by the time Reizel and Dena were safely over the wall, he had disappeared.

Who could the stranger be? Everybody offered guesses—except Esther, who wondered most of all. It was Reizel who solved the mystery. A few days after the rescue she came into the house bursting with importance.

"Do you know who the boy is who saved us from the dogs? His name is Leib. He's visiting Buna Sasha's, whose husband has the oil press. She's his aunt."

A dramatic pause, then the climax. "He's a son of Fraida whose father died when she was born."

The excitement that followed was enough to satisfy even Reizel.

"How do you know?"

113

"Who told you?"

"*He* did," said Reizel. "I met him in the market, so I thanked him, of course. And he said it was nothing. I asked him his name and where he lived, and he asked me my name. . . ." She turned to Esther. "He asked me *your* name, too. When I told him 'Esther,' do you know what he said?"

Esther shrugged, as if it made no difference.

"All right, then I won't tell," Reizel said.

"So tell," said Esther.

"He said, 'Like Esther the Queen. The name fits her.'"

"Like Esther the Queen!" The children chanted it in chorus until Momme threatened to give each of them a good slap on the cheek if they didn't stop teasing.

For days, they whispered under their breath, "The name fits her."

Esther scarcely noticed. Suddenly—she could not tell why—she found herself moving in a golden haze. All the family, Father, Momme, the girls, Kezele, Dovidel the baby, were enveloped in its warm golden glow.

After the Three Weeks of mourning comes the Sabbath of Comfort. On Sabbath afternoon the family was sitting in the doorway when who should turn into their lane but the very one who was in Esther's thoughts, the young stranger, Leib.

Reizel raced across the street and brought him over to the family.

"Good Sabbath," they greeted him.

"Good Sabbath," he answered awkwardly, looking at everyone except Esther.

"It gives me pleasure to meet Fraida's son," said Momme. "How is your mother's health?"

"She is well, thank God. Thank you for asking."

"And your father?" Momme inquired.

"He, too, is well."

Reizel interrupted the polite talk.

"Leib," she asked, "will you teach me the words that make dogs stop barking?"

At Leib's puzzled look, she added, "The words with the letters of the Holy Name. I heard you say them."

Leib's eyes crinkled in a smile.

"You heard me say Zaager and Aazman," he said, laughing, at ease at last. "I was calling the dogs by their names. They know me."

Goldie gave Reizel an I-told-you-so look.

Now Fayge asked a question.

"Is it true that there are trees carved on the cup your uncle sent from Jerusalem?"

"Yes," said Leib. "They rise from behind the wailing wall."

"Are they like our trees?"

"No," Leib explained gravely, "the trees in the Holy City point to heaven."

After this everybody joined in the talk—except Esther. It was enough for her to listen. Sometimes she glanced toward their visitor, only to discover that his eyes were on her. She lowered her own eyes quickly.

Suddenly Leib seemed to realize that he might be staying too long.

"I must go on," he said, awkward again. "I am on my way to the synagogue. It was fortunate that I happened to pass your home."

He wished them a good Sabbath and was off.

Father waited until Leib had turned into the square. Then he laughed aloud. "His aunt lives on the other side of town and he happened to pass our house on his way to the synagogue. Next time he will go to the synagogue by way of America."

Father turned to Momme.

"Gittel," he said, "our Esther is no longer a child. We shall have to begin thinking in earnest about a dowry."

"And feather beds," thought Momme.

Jacob's Well

IT WAS A GOOD THING that Reizel had her friend Dena to talk to. Otherwise she would have burst with all the thoughts about Gadya that crowded her mind. True, Reizel talked about him to the family. But talking to the family about Gadya was not very satisfying. Father laughed. Momme listened, but answered neither one way nor another. Esther and Fayge said, "Do you think so? It may be." But Reizel could tell they considered her a baby. Kezele and the twins were too young. It was better with Goldie. But the best one to talk to was Dena.

Dena not only agreed with Reizel's ideas about Gadya, she gave her new ones. There was the day Father said, "Do you think Elijah has nothing more important to do than bother about a kid?"

Reizel told Dena about it, and Dena told her the story of Moses' lamb. The little lamb ran away, and Moses, who was a shepherd, had to go after it. On and on Moses went under the burning sun, until he found the lamb lapping water from a stream. Do you think he scolded it? No! He said, "Poor lamb, you must have been very thirsty to come this long way.

117

You are tired." And he picked the lamb up and carried it home on his shoulders.

"If Moses, our Teacher, troubled himself about a lamb, Elijah can bother about a kid," Dena said.

Dena had learned the story about Moses in her Bible class at school. Reizel had not yet begun school, but Dena had been going since she was six years old.

Dena always said that Reizel was lucky to have so many sisters and brothers. But there was one thing not so lucky about it. You had to take turns. First Esther had gone to school, then Fayge and Esther. Now it was Goldie's turn. Father said that schooling for two children was all that he could manage at one time. School had to be paid for. Dena, who had only a baby brother and one little sister, didn't have to wait. She could read "like water," flowingly.

Reizel's biggest wish was to go to school and learn how to read.

"If you want it so much," Dena said one day, "why don't you wish out loud when Gadya hears you? He has given all the others their wishes, and he's *your* kid."

"There he is now," she said, as Gadya poked his nose around the corner of the house. "Wish quick!"

So Reizel did, and the very next day she discovered *Jacob's Well*.

Jacob's Well was not a well from which one draws water. It was a book full of stories from the *Talmud,* the teachings of the ancient rabbis. Fathers studied it in the synagogue between afternoon and evening prayers. Reizel learned about *Jacob's Well* when Dena was sent to the House of Study with a message for her father, and asked her to go along. At the door, Reizel happened to look back. There was Gadya following them.

"I'll wait outside and watch him," Reizel said.

But Gadya didn't want to stay outside. Before Reizel could stop him he had slipped into the synagogue. Reizel found him behind a bench near a big table where a group of men were studying. She crouched down beside him, waiting for a chance to get him out without starting a commotion. Then she grew so interested in what the teacher at the table was saying, she completely forgot about the kid.

The lesson was about a prophet named Joel. A dreadful time came, a time of famine. People went to the prophet and said, "What if a man has no more than a measure of wheat or two measures of barley? Shall he eat it and live, or plant it and die?"

The prophet said, "Nevertheless, go out and plant."

They began to do as he had said, when a miracle happened. Grain, hidden by mice in walls and by ants in cracks and in anthills, suddenly appeared before their eyes. They planted it and a great crop sprang up. Therefore . . .

At this point Dena returned and Gadya jumped up and ran after her. So Reizel had to leave.

All day she kept wondering just how the grain

119

hidden by the mice and the ants had appeared. Did the walls crack open? Did the grain come marching out of the hills like ants in a row?

"Maybe," she thought, "the ants themselves brought the seeds."

She could see them in a long line, each bearing a kernel of grain.

The next day Reizel went back to the House of Study in the hope that she might hear the end of the story. She didn't. But she learned other things—for instance, that in the Land of Israel there are early rains and latter rains. The early rains were called *yoreh,* to teach, because they taught men to plaster their roofs, gather in their fruits, and make all other preparations for the winter. *Jacob's Well* didn't say what the other preparations were, but Reizel knew. Soon they, too, would be making them. She could see the people cutting turf near the bog where the cranberries grew. She could see them storing sacks of potatoes, enough for the family and the goat, and to cut up and plant in the spring. She could see them burying cabbages and carrots and turnips in mounds of sand, where the frost would not reach them.

After this Reizel went to the House of Study almost every afternoon. Dena would keep Gadya from following her. Reizel would stand behind a bench where she could hear without being seen. First the teacher would read the lesson in Hebrew. Then he would explain what he had read. Sometimes the lesson was so dull and hard to understand that Reizel made up her mind not to come back any more. Then right in the dullest part a story would come up—like the one about *Rabbi Joshua and the Princess.*

Ten and a Kid

Rabbi Joshua was good and wise, but very homely. Once the princess said to him, "How can precious wisdom live in such an ugly head?"

Rabbi Joshua said to her, "My daughter, in what sort of vessels does your father keep his wine?"

"In earthen jars," she answered. "Where *should* he keep it?"

Rabbi Joshua said, "Should not a King keep his wine in vessels of gold and silver?"

The princess went to her father and asked him to have the wine poured into gold and silver vessels. Of course, the wine spoiled.

Then the King said to Rabbi Joshua, "Why did you give my daughter this advice?"

Rabbi Joshua replied, "It was to answer her question. Now she will understand that precious things can be found in ugly containers."

The story made Reizel feel better about not having golden curls like Goldie's. Rabbi Joshua had lived over a thousand years ago, but Reizel felt as if he were her own rabbi. She wished that she could ask Father whether Rabbi Joshua's feelings had been hurt by the princess' rude question. She liked Rabbi Joshua. But if Father found out that she was listening to the class in *Jacob's Well*, he was sure to tease her, and Reizel didn't feel like being teased.

Only Dena knew her secret. They talked about it in whispers. Dena would help her slip away to the House of Study without anyone knowing it. It was mysterious and exciting to have a secret.

But one day Reizel, herself, let the secret slip. It happened at the supper table when Teppele choked over her soup.

"That comes from talking while you eat," Father said.

"That's just what it says in *Jacob's Well,*" Reizel chimed in. "It says, 'Rabbi Johanon taught that one must not talk while eating lest the windpipe open and endanger one's life.'"

Father turned to Reizel in surprise.

"Where did you learn what is written in *Jacob's Well?*" he asked.

Without thinking, Reizel answered, "At the class in the House of Study."

Her secret was out!

The teasing followed just as she had expected.

"Have you heard, Gittel?" Father said. "Our daughter is now a member of the class in *Jacob's Well!*"

After this Reizel stopped going to *Jacob's Well*. But she didn't stop wanting to learn to read. Hearing the stories had made her want to read more than ever.

"What's the letter with the long neck?" she would

123

ask Momme, pointing to a *Lamed* in her prayer book. "What's the little dot up in the air?" she would ask Esther.

The end was that everyone began teaching Reizel: Momme, Esther, Fayge, Dena, even Goldie.

A Sabbath came when Goldie and Reizel went up to the women's gallery in the synagogue. Momme was reading the prayers aloud for the women who could not read by themselves. She beckoned to Goldie, and pointed to the place in the prayer book. But it wasn't Goldie who read. *Reizel* read for Momme—a whole page, slowly, but with only a few mistakes. Momme kissed her right in the synagogue.

"Reizel," Dena said to her when the service was over, "do you remember when you made your wish in front of Gadya? Well, now you can read."

"Only in the prayer book," Reizel answered. "But it's a beginning," she admitted.

Her eyes brightened.

"When I can read *Jacob's Well,*" she said, "I'll skip all the dull places, and go straight to the stories."

In The Sukkah

THE SOLEMN FALL HOLY DAYS had come and gone; *Rosh Hashonah,* the New Year, Day of the Blowing of the *Shofar,* the ram's horn; *Yom Kippur,* day of fasting and of asking forgiveness. Now *Sukkos,* the joyful festival of Thanksgiving, was at hand. From the back yard came a sound of hammering. Father was building a *sukkah,* a little hut covered with green boughs, to remind them of the frail huts the children of Israel built when they wandered in the wilderness for forty years.

In the kitchen the girls were blowing out eggs for Fayge to turn into eggshell birds. Only Reizel's hands were idle.

"Do you know what I think?" Reizel spoke up suddenly. "I think we could very well do without a *sukkah.*"

Nobody looked shocked. The family was used to Reizel's outbursts.

"What's wrong with a *sukkah?*" Fayge asked quietly.

She herself thought that nothing was so lovely as a *sukkah* with its covering of green branches. No roof to shut out the sky! Red apples, yellow pears, clusters of purple grapes hung from the boughs. At night the stars shone through.

125

"I should think you'd be glad to sit in a *sukkah,*" Fayge said.

"That's just the trouble. Girls *don't* sit in the *sukkah.* Only boys and men do. Boys get everything. They don't have to wait their turn to go to school. They sit in the *sukkah.* It's not fair."

None of them could deny Reizel's words. Kezele was to begin school right after the holidays, though he would not be five years old for another month. As for the *sukkah,* the law said, "Women are not required to observe the commandment of the *sukkah.*" So, on *Sukkos,* Father and Kezele, with a guest or two, ate in the *sukkah* while Momme and the girls ran back and forth waiting on them.

"Who gets the food when it's good and hot?" Reizel demanded. "*They* do. Who gets what's left over? *We* do."

This, too, could not be denied. Teppele's thoughts turned back to last year's festival. She could see Momme in the kitchen lifting the cover from a pot of *tsimmes.* Steam arose. It smelled of carrots and dumplings and bits of fat meat, all sweetened, and stewing gently in their juices. The smell teased Teppele's nose.

"Give us a taste, Momme," she begged.

But Momme clapped the cover on again. "What sort of talk is this? Carry the *tsimmes* out to the *sukkah* before it gets cold."

Reizel's voice brought Teppele back to the present.

"*Tsimmes* is my favorite food," she was saying, as if she had read Teppele's thoughts.

"And you get plenty of it on *Sukkos,*" said Esther. "You ought to be ashamed of yourself, Reizel, talking as if Father ate the whole *tsimmes* himself."

But Reizel would not be silenced.

"I don't like *tsimmes* when it's cold. Besides, by the time it comes back to us, the best pieces of dumpling are picked out."

The twins nodded in agreement. One could see that they were beginning to feel sorry for themselves. Reizel offered another complaint.

"Father sings so much. He sings every song he knows."

This, too, was true. Father gathered in the joy of all the Sabbaths and festivals and poured it into the songs he sang in the *sukkah,* songs in Hebrew and in Yiddish, songs of thanks and praise.

"But I thought you liked Father's songs," said Goldie. "You join in louder than I do at the Sabbath table."

Goldie, you remember, was the song bird of the family. Reizel's singing was what Father called "a joyful noise unto the Lord."

"I do like singing," Reizel explained. "It's the *waiting* I don't like."

Again the children knew what Reizel meant. It was one thing to sing when one's stomach was warm and full, and another when the food grew colder and

127

one's stomach emptier with every verse. And some of the songs had a verse for every letter of the alphabet.

Luckily, Father called to the children at that moment.

"Come out, someone. I need help."

He was up on a ladder, covering the top of the *sukkah* with green branches.

With a final "It isn't fair," Reizel ran out to Father.

All this happened on a Friday morning. On Sabbath afternoon Reizel sat curled up on a bench, listening to Momme and their friend Hannah Rachel talking together. Whenever their neighbor came over, Reizel listened. You remember that Hannah Rachel came from a distant mountain village and had strange stories to tell, stories of evil spirits that

roamed the forests in the form of wolves, stories of saints and holy men. On this Sabbath she spoke, not of a holy man, but of a holy woman after whom she had been named, the Holy Maid of Ludimer. Every morning, Hannah Rachel said, this holy woman wrapped herself in a *tallis* and put on *tefillin.*

Reizel heard her in astonishment. A *tallis* is a prayer shawl; *tefillin* are small leather cubes containing verses from the Holy Bible. One cube is strapped to the forehead, one to the right arm opposite the heart, a reminder to keep God's law in one's heart and in one's thoughts. Father always wore them at his morning prayers. But Momme never did. Praying in a prayer shawl and *tefillin* was a commandment, a *mitzvah,* for men, not for women.

Now you can understand Reizel's astonishment. A WOMAN, the Holy Maid of Ludimer, had worn a *tallis* and *tefillin* and been praised for it! An idea flashed through Reizel's mind. As soon as Father returned from the synagogue she asked him about the maid.

"How does it come, Father, that a woman put on *tallis* and *tefillin* which is a man's *mitzvah?*"

"Why do you want to know?" Father asked. His eyes twinkled. "Are you planning to become a Holy Maid? So far there has been only one."

"I have asked you a question and you should answer it, not tease me."

"You are right," said Father, and he answered her

in the singing tones in which scholars explained a point in the *Talmud*.

"The law says a man is required to put on *tefillin*. It does not say that a woman is not permitted. A woman is excused. But if the Maid of Ludimer did not want to be excused, if she preferred to take on the commandment, what was to prevent her?"

Father's twinkle returned.

"If you are thinking of putting on *tallis* and *tefillin*, Reizel, you will have to wait a while. Even a boy must wait until he is thirteen."

But Reizel was not interested in *tefillin*. It was the *sukkah* she was thinking of.

"Does the Torah say a woman *may* not sit in the *sukkah,* or does it say she *need* not?"

"It says she *need* not," Father answered.

Reizel's eyes danced.

"Father," she said nobly, "the women in our family do not want to be excused. We will take on ourselves the duty of sitting in the *sukkah*."

So it came about that on the festival, *all* Avrom Itsik's family ate in the *sukkah*. True, Momme was out of the *sukkah* more than she was in it. True, the sisters jumped up and down bringing in the food. But after they had brought it in, they could eat it, warm and savory. The pine boughs overhead sent down a spicy fragrance. The sky looked in through the openings, bluer than when one saw it out of doors. Fayge's eggshell birds twirled slowly on their strings.

What did it matter if dampness rose from the ground? The singing warmed them. Reizel would not have minded if the alphabet had a hundred letters.

"Gadya," Reizel said, as she fed the little kid leftovers from the *sukkah* meal, "I'm so full of gladness, I don't suppose I could hold another bit— unless, of course, Father let me go to school."

She looked into Gadya's golden eyes. The pupils narrowed into mysterious slits. Were they hiding a secret?

In the Sukkah

Rejoice and Be Glad

THE SEASON OF GLADNESS, which began with *Sukkos,* ended with *Simchas Torah,* the rejoicing in God's Law. On *Simchas Torah* the last portion in the *Torah* was read. Then the scroll was rolled back to the beginning, and the reading started again.

All the *Torah* scrolls, beautiful in their velvet mantles and silver ornaments, were taken from the Ark. Silver breastplates gleamed. Bells on the crowns tinkled. Seven times the scrolls were borne in glad processions around the synagogue. Fathers took turns carrying them. Mothers and older sisters came down from the gallery and crowded into the aisles to touch them lovingly as they passed. Children followed, singing and waving flags.

> Rejoice and be glad!
> Rejoice and be glad!

Reizel, circling the synagogue for the seventh time, wished that Gadya were beside her. She could

133

see him dancing on his delicate hind legs, his horns like tiny *shofars,* his tail waving like a banner.

In front of her, Kezele was waving his new flag. Father had given him a new one because he was to begin school right after *Simchas Torah.* There was a Hebrew verse on the flag, and the picture of a lion standing on its hind legs the way Gadya did. Father had read Kezele the verse before they left for the synagogue.

> *Be swift as a deer and strong as a lion,*
> *To do the will of your Father in Heaven.*

Reizel was sure that she would be "swift as a deer and strong as a lion" to study *Torah,* if only she could go to school. But she was not going. Kezele was going. Thinking about *not* going to school wasn't very gladdening. Reizel turned her thoughts back to *Simchas Torah.*

> *Rejoice and be glad,* she sang.
> *Rejoice and be glad!*

On the morning after *Simchas Torah,* Father brought Reb Gershon, the teacher, home with him from services. Kezele was to start school the next day. The family didn't call it "school." They called it *heder.* This wasn't the school that Fayge and Goldie went to. Theirs was only for girls.

Momme said that all teachers were poor, but that Reb Gershon was the poorest of them all. People

Rejoice and Be Glad

135

called him a saint. They said that he taught *Torah* all day and studied *Torah* all night. But most of them sent their sons to the other *heder,* Reb Mottel Lazer's. They said that Reb Gershon "spared the rod."

Reizel knew, from listening to the *heder* boys, that Reb Mottel never spared the rod. A leather strap with three stinging tails hung on his wall. You had to be very brave not to cry out when the strap came down on you. Kezele's sisters were glad that he was going to Reb Gershon's *heder,* not Reb Mottel's.

It was exciting to Reizel to have a teacher in their own house. She watched him, as Kezele recited the blessings over the wine and honey cake that Momme brought to the table. Reb Gershon made her think of the letter *Vov,* tall and thin, his shoulders a little stooped, his head bent forward, listening. She thought he would be a good person for answering questions. His smile didn't seem like the teasing kind.

Now Reb Gershon opened a prayer book and told Kezele to look into it. Kezele bent his head, and three copper coins fell on the page.

"Take them," Reb Gershon said to the delighted Kezele. "The angels dropped them down for you because you are a fine boy and are going to study *Torah.*"

Reizel had seen Reb Gershon, himself, drop the coins on the page, but she didn't tell. She edged closer to the table.

"Is this the one who learned to read by herself?" Reb Gershon asked Momme.

When Momme answered that it was, he asked Reizel to read for him. She did, her heart thumping.

"The angels ought to drop gifts down for this one also," Reb Gershon said to Father.

Next morning, very early, Father wrapped Kezele in a prayer shawl and carried him to school. All the family went along.

Reb Gershon's house was even smaller than their own. It had a thatched roof and one room. His wife, Zissel, was preparing breakfast. With one hand she stirred a pot, with the other she rocked the cradle. In the center of the room was a long table with benches for the pupils who had not yet arrived.

"Well, Moshe ben Avraham," Reb Gershon said, calling Kezele by his full Hebrew name, "are you ready for your first lesson?"

He handed Kezele a paper on which Hebrew verses had been written. *The letters were covered with honey.*

"Lick them," Reb Gershon said.

Kezele licked.

"Are they sweet?"

"Sweet!"

"Like God's teachings," said Reb Gershon. "Now say the verse after me. 'Sweeter are they.'"

"Sweeter are they," Kezele repeated.

"Than honey and the honeycomb."

"Than honey and the honeycomb."

"More to be desired are they than fine gold," Reb Gershon continued.

"More to be desired than fine gold," Kezele said dutifully.

It was right after this that Reizel heard words which to her were sweeter than honey and the honeycomb.

"Reizel," Father said, "your mother and I have been talking with Reb Gershon. You are to go to *heder* with Kezele every day—someone must take him back and forth. While you are here, you will study with the second class. Reb Gershon has never taken a girl before; but he says that a child who finds her way into a book without a teacher deserves to have a teacher to take her further."

A gleam came into Father's eyes. "Now don't go thanking Gadya for this. Reb Gershon is the one to thank. Well, Reizel, what have you to say?"

For once Reizel said nothing. The joy that welled up from her heart could not possibly be squeezed into words. Her eyes thanked them, Father, Momme, Reb Gershon. They fell on Zissel, Reb Gershon's wife. She was holding the baby in her arms. Four other little ones clung to her skirts.

Suddenly words poured forth. "I'll help you, Zissel Gershon's. I can rock the baby while I learn. I'll sweep and do lots of things."

She turned to Reb Gershon. "You'll be glad you took me."

A thump on the roof sent Reizel flying through the door. It was as she thought. Gadya had climbed on the roof and was chewing at the thatch.

"Come down, Gadya," Reizel called. "You deserve a good meal, but not the *rebbi's* roof."

The little kid jumped down and ran over to her. He looked up into her eyes as if asking whether she were pleased.

Rejoice and Be Glad

"Thank you, Gadya," Reizel whispered, forgetting what Father had said. "You've given me another wish, the biggest one of all."

The Sabbath Pots

EVERY FRIDAY AFTERNOON the children carried five earthen pots to Frume Leah's kitchen. There they were sealed into the big oven and kept warm for the Sabbath meal next day, when cooking and kindling fires were not permitted. Three of the pots were their own. Two belonged to Mume Bryna who was too old and feeble to carry them herself. The children thought that she must be at least a hundred years old. Once Reizel tried to see whether she could find one place on Mume's face without a wrinkle, but she couldn't.

Teppele's favorite task was calling for the Sabbath pots after the service on Saturday morning. She liked to see them drawn out of the oven with the long, hooked stick. She liked the feel of the pots, the good warmth that came through the cloth wrappings. She liked the game they played on the way home.

"What's in my pot?" one of the children would begin.

141

"Roast goose," someone answered.

"Egg barley with chicken breasts," said another.

"Stuffed goose necks!"

No one tried to guess what was really in the pots. The game was to mention what they *wished* were in the pot.

But what the pots contained was mouth-watering enough.

Teppele always managed to be near when Momme lifted the covers and the first whiff of steam arose. The potatoes were brown and crisp, the peas and barley thick from long cooking, the soup hot and flavorful, all the goodness sealed in. Sometimes, when Father had had an especially good week, there was a sweet stew or a fat pudding.

Mume Bryna sent only two pots, one with peas and barley and one with soup. She said that her stomach was too weak for rich foods. Her pots were the lightest, so Teppele and Tseppele carried them.

It was in this way, one Friday, that Teppele happened to look into Mume Bryna's soup pot. Mume wasn't in the kitchen when Teppele came in. The pots were on the table ready to be taken to the oven. Teppele didn't mean to be inquisitive. Looking into pots was a habit with her. What she saw made her leave the pots standing on the table while she rushed home to Momme.

"Momme," she cried, "Mume has no meat for *Shabbos*." *Shabbos* was what they called their Sabbath.

"Are you sure?" asked Momme.

"I saw. There was only water and an onion and a bay leaf in the pot—no chicken, no meat bones, nothing!"

Teppele's voice was full of distress. The children were very fond of Mume Bryna. Having her across the street was almost like having a grandmother nearby.

"Momme," Teppele asked, "can't we give Mume a piece of *our* chicken, a wing or something?"

"It's not so easy," said Momme. "If Mume wanted us to know that she had no meat for *Shabbos,* she wouldn't be sending a pot with nothing but water in it to the bake oven. It is better for Mume to keep her pride than to have a chicken wing."

"I could slip it into the pot without her knowing," said Teppele. "She can hardly see. When I come into her house, she says, 'Is that you, Teppele my life?'"

"But Teppele," Momme spoke gently. "She would know when it came to the eating."

Reizel came to Teppele's support.

"Mume might think a miracle happened the way it did to Rabbi Hanina's wife. They were so poor she didn't even have flour to bake bread. So, on Friday, she burned sticks in the oven to make smoke go up so the neighbors wouldn't know. But one neighbor, who was always minding other people's business, said, 'I'm sure that she has nothing to bake for *Shabbos*. What can be causing the smoke?'

"She went into Rabbi Hanina's house to see. *The kneading trough was full of dough. The oven was full of bread.*

"'Come quickly,' she called to Rabbi Hanina's wife who was in the other room. 'Bring a shovel or your bread will burn.'

"Rabbi Hanina's wife came running with a shovel. She knew that a miracle had happened."

Reizel ended the story dramatically. Next to hearing a story, she liked nothing better than telling one.

"Mume might also think a miracle happened," Reizel added.

Father, who was already home and preparing for the Sabbath, spoke up. "Rabbi Hanina's wife was used to miracles. Mume would not recognize a miracle if she saw one. She hasn't been a member of the class in *Jacob's Well* as you have, Reizel. I'm afraid Mume will have to do with peas and barley this Sabbath."

But Momme thought otherwise.

"Wait here," she said to the children.

She threw a shawl over her head and went over to Mume's house.

"Bryna," she asked, "can you, perhaps, spare a little meat? A small piece will do. I am short this Sabbath."

Mume Bryna hesitated, embarrassed. "I am sorry, Gittel. You know that I would give it to you gladly. But it happens that I myself have no meat this Sabbath."

"Why didn't you tell me?" said Momme. "I will send over a bit of ours. Where there is not enough in the first place, a little less will make no great difference."

Momme was already out of the door.

What was Mume Bryna to do? Could she follow Momme and say, "Gittel, you are making a beggar out of me." It would be like calling Momme a beggar, since she herself had come to borrow a piece of meat.

Suddenly Mume found herself amused rather than troubled.

"May no greater misfortune happen to either of us," she murmured, laughing.

At home, Momme was spooning a meaty bone and a chicken wing out of the soup pot. She put them into a covered dish.

"Take this to Mume Bryna," Momme said to Teppele.

145

"How did you? . . ." Teppele began.

"Do as I say, and ask no questions," Momme said, closing the subject.

But her eyes smiled. She bent over and kissed Teppele on the forehead.

"Teppele," Reizel said later in the day when only Gadya was listening, "how could you tell there was nothing in Mume's pot? Did you take off the cover? Just tell *me*."

"I didn't. Honestly!" Teppele protested. "It was Gadya. He jumped on Mume's table and pushed the cover off."

Reizel's face broke into a smile.

"Of course," she said. "Gadya wanted to make sure that Mume had a proper meal for *Shabbos*. He's taking care of her because she was at our *seder* table. Remember?"

The Wish of Momme's Heart

FALL RAINS CHURNED the dust of the lane into mud. Frost hardened it into deep ruts. Now the winds brought flurries of snow.

Inside, turf burned all day in the big clay oven. Double windows, with sand between the panes, shut out the wind. Gay little cornucopias of colored paper were stuck into the sand. In the shed, Father had filled in the chinks and piled up straw for a warm bed for Gadya. But the little kid preferred to be in the house.

Momme did not mind. With all the children except the twins in school, she was glad to have Gadya amuse the baby. Dovidel's sober little face would light up when he spied the kid. He would crawl over to him quickly, the corners of his mouth turned up, his cheeks rounding out like two rosy apples. Momme could trust Gadya to be gentle with Dovidel. But Dovidel was not always gentle with Gadya. He was too fond of grabbing things, handfuls of Momme's hair, Goldie's curls, Gadya's tail or horns, or silken tassels.

It was to get away from Dovidel that Gadya climbed on top of the oven one day—the chimney part, not the cooking part—and discovered that it

147

was the warmest place in the house. After that, it became Gadya's favorite spot. Reizel often climbed up beside him when she returned from school. It was in this way that she overheard Father and Momme talking together one Friday afternoon.

School was dismissed at noon on Fridays. The rest of the children were sliding on the frozen lake. But a story in the week's Bible portion had sent Reizel hurrying home to Gadya. The story told of wild beasts which lurked in the forests, waiting to spring on a little lamb or kid and tear it to pieces. Jacob, the good shepherd, had to keep watch night and day, even in bitter frost. It was comforting to Reizel to find Gadya curled up safely on the oven top. She had her arms around him protectively when Father came into the house, stamping the snow from his boots.

"Gittel," he said as Momme poured him a glass of tea, "our young man is in town again. I saw him coming out of Buna Sasha's house. Suddenly he has grown very devoted to his relatives. This is the second time he has visited them since he met our Esther."

Father laughed. "Leib's grandfather married a dowerless bride. If Leib wants our Esther, he will have to do as his grandfather did."

"Maybe a bride without a dowry," Momme said, "but not without bedding. How can one send a daughter away without so much as pillows and feather beds? It isn't seemly. Avrom, try to be seri-

ous," she pleaded. "Where are we going to get feathers?"

"Feathers! Always feathers! What do you want me to do, Gittel? Bring them down for you on a platter from heaven?"

Father pushed back his glass of tea and stalked into the bedroom. Momme followed.

Reizel turned to the little kid. "Gadya," she said, "you have given all of us our wishes. Can't you give Momme hers? Please, Gadya, try! It's very important."

Gadya nodded his head soberly. Reizel was sure that all would be well. But days passed, weeks passed, and no feathers appeared. Soon a new month would begin, the month of *Kislev*. And still there were no feathers.

On the Sabbath before the new moon, Momme gathered the children around her for the blessing of the coming month.

May it be Thy will, O Lord our God and the God of our fathers, to renew unto us this coming month for good and for blessing. O grant us long life, a life of peace, of goodness, of health . . .

The prayer went on and on, ending, *a life in which the wishes of our hearts will be fulfilled for good.*

Reizel's heart was sad as she listened. She knew the wish of Momme's heart, and it had not been fulfilled.

Gadya, standing beside her, tried to hide his head in her skirts.

"I'm not blaming you, Gadya. It isn't your fault," Reizel assured him. "I guess getting Momme her feathers is too hard for a kid, even Elijah's kid."

The sadness stayed on throughout the day. Toward evening fresh snow began falling. Once Father had told Reizel that when snow fell the German children across the border would say, "The old woman in the sky is shaking her feather beds."

"Maybe these *are* feathers," Reizel thought as she watched the feathery flakes come down through the dusk. "Maybe Gadya got them for Momme after all."

But she dismissed the notion quickly. There wasn't any old woman in the sky. It was God who sent the snow.

Esther had been looking up at the sky through the window. Now she announced that she could see three stars.

Softly, Momme began chanting the God of Abraham prayer.

The sweet and holy Sabbath nears its end.
Now, in Thy loving kindness, send
A week of life and health, of bread and savor,
Honest gains, strength for our daily labor,
To us, all Israel, to good folk everywhere.
Dear God, my little ones, I place within Thy care.
May they be pure and righteous,
Worthy of Thy favor.

151

She turned toward the door, her voice rising strong and sure.

> *Elijah the prophet is at our door.*
> *Let all that is evil keep away,*
> *All good come in and stay,*
> *Now and forever more.*

Ten and a Kid

"Elijah the prophet is at our door!" The words echoed in Reizel's heart. Of course! Elijah came at the close of the Sabbath just as he did on *seder* night. Didn't they sing to him, when Father returned from the synagogue, *Elijah the Prophet, Elijah the Tishbite, Elijah the Gileadite!*

Reizel knew what she must do. She would speak to Elijah again as she had spoken to him on Passover. She would explain how important it was for Momme to get the feathers, and ask him to help his little kid.

The rest of the family were busy with Dovidel who had chosen that moment to show them how he made patty cakes. Reizel threw a shawl over herself and slipped out through the door.

"Elijah," she whispered into the night, "thank you for sending us your little kid. He is so precious, we would love him even if he didn't do wonders. But he does do wonders. He has given all of us our wishes—except Momme. Feathers are too hard for him. Momme needs the feathers for Esther. It's very important. Please, Elijah, help Gadya to get them for her."

152

She paused, then added, "You don't have to do it this minute, Elijah. Just when you have time."

A star came falling through the night. Was it a sign that Elijah had heard her?

Reizel felt Gadya pressing against her skirts.

"It will be all right, Gadya," she said to him, her voice glad and sure. "Elijah will help you."

The Wish of Momme's Heart

Hanukah Is Coming

SNOW FELL ON SNOW, crusting over into mounds of sparkling white sugar with little sugar-capped houses and a white sugar path.

This is how the lane looked to Fayge as she stood near the window, watching Momme make a *Hanukah* lamp. It was a potato *Hanukah* lamp. Momme took eight smooth potatoes, all of a size, cut a hole in each one big enough to hold a *Hanukah* candle, and set them in a row in the window. Then she added a smaller potato for the *shammas,* the candle that kindles all the others. One candle would be lit on the first night, two on the second, an added candle each night until all eight were burning.

"There," said Momme. "We have a good, firm holder for our *Hanukah* lights."

"I wish we had the one with the lions," said Goldie. She meant the brass lamp that was sold the year the twins were born. "I wish we had a silver lamp—or a GOLD one."

Father looked up from a bit of wood he was carving.

"And why," he asked, "is a lump of hard gold better than a potato? In Sodom and Gomorah . . ."

Everybody listened. When Father mentioned the wicked cities of Sodom and Gomorah, they knew that a story was coming.

"In Sodom and Gomorah," said Father, "there was gold without measure. So what happened? If a stranger lost his way and came there, the wicked ones served him food made of gold—bread, meat, fish, fowl, all of hard gold. Nothing else! Can a man eat gold? The stranger died of hunger.

"Now, if they had given the stranger a potato! Ah, a potato! You take a scrap of peeling with an eye in it, and bury it in the ground. Greens come up. Roots go down. They bring forth fruit, nuggets brown as God's earth, something to nourish a man. Potatoes!"

Father turned toward the row of potatoes in the window, and the eyes of the children turned with him. A sunbeam slanted through a pane. Suddenly Momme's potato lamp gleamed with a heavenly light.

Only Reizel was unimpressed.

"If a potato lamp is so fine," she asked, "why did they have a gold one in the Holy Temple?"

But Father had gone back to his carving. He was making a *dreidle,* a *Hanukah* top with a Hebrew letter on each side. *Nes Godol Hoyoh Shom,* the letters declared—"A Great Miracle Happened There." *There,* of course, was Jerusalem in days of old when the wicked King Antiochus rose up to make the Jews forget God's holy laws. Even Kezele knew the story, but he begged Momme to read it to them again. So she did, out of a big book; how Antiochus, the madman, siezed the Holy Temple and put out the Eternal Light, the light that must always be kept burning. But the brave Judah Maccabee and his brothers saved the Temple from his hands, and cleansed it, and kindled the light again.

"Only one jar of pure oil could be found, no more than would keep the light burning for a day," Momme read, "but God sent down his blessing and the oil burned for *eight* days. Wherefore we celebrate this season with joy and gladness and kindle lights in all the houses for eight days."

"And spin *dreidles*," Kezele added. "Make me a *lucky dreidle*, Father."

"Did I ever make an unlucky one?" Father asked. He was an expert at making *dreidles*. He made them for Kezele and the girls and all their friends.

But Father, himself, did not know how lucky a *dreidle* of his could be. That very day he was to make one that would spin and spin until it spun them *Hanukah* coins and potato pancakes and sacks full of . . . You will soon know what they were full of.

Does it seem to you impossible that a *dreidle* should do all this? It did not seem impossible to Reizel. Reizel was expecting wonders.

It all began that afternoon when the door opened wide and Reizel came in, her cheeks red with cold and excitement. Gadya was at her heels.

"A blessing on you, Reizel! Shut the door, quick," Momme said, her voice sounding more like a scolding than a blessing. "How often must I tell you not to drag in the cold!"

Reizel was too full of her news to mind.

"Do you know what happened, Momme?" she said, running on all in one breath. "I was coming home across the square and Gadya turned around and ran the wrong way, so I had to run after him and I bumped right into Frume Leah. But she didn't scold. She said, 'Wait until I get my breath, Reizel.' Then she asked me if Father didn't make *dreidles,* so I said he did, and she told me to ask him if he would do her the kindness to make one for her little grandson Yossie. He is coming to them for *Hanukah.* Will you make one, Father?"

Father said of course he would make Frume Leah a *dreidle.* And what a *dreidle!* A *dreidle* such as they

had never seen! Didn't they use Frume Leah's mangle every spring? Wasn't it to her kitchen they brought their Sabbath pots each Friday? Now he could do something for her and her little grandson.

The children hung over Father as he worked. He chose the wood carefully. He cut and shaped and whittled. The *dreidle* took form; a sturdy four-sided body, a twirler at the top, the bottom curving inward, tapering to a fine point. Father examined it, turned it this way and that, tried it out. The balance must be perfect. Now he took a stone and rubbed the wood satin smooth. Next he outlined the Hebrew letters, one on each side. Carefully, carefully, he cut the wood from around them until the letters stood out bold and beautiful like the letters in a holy scroll.

The children hovered over the table as Father gave the *dreidle* its first spin. Round and round it whirled, round and round, faster and faster and faster. It was no longer a *dreidle*. It was a whirr of light. The *dreidle* stopped at last—not suddenly, but swaying gently like one at prayer.

"Well, Gittel, will it do?" Father asked.

Momme's eyes filled with pride in her husband.

That night, after Father had kindled the first light and everyone had sung "We thank Thee for the miracles and saving acts," Momme bundled Kezele, the twins, Reizel, and Goldie into warm coats and shawls and mufflers, and sent them to Frume Leah's house with the *dreidle*. They set out single file along

Hanukah Is Coming

159

the snowy path. The *Hanukah* lights in the houses made little blurs of light on the frosty panes.

Across the quiet square to Frume Leah's yard the children hurried, past the snow-covered sheds and the shadowy piles of logs, up the three steps. Natasha, the servant woman, opened the door. Even on *Hanukah* her sleeves were rolled up and her big arms covered with flour. Natasha took the *dreidle* from Kezele's hand, and left the children standing in the hallway. In a few minutes she returned with an envelope.

"The mistress says it is a beautiful *dreidle*. She thanks your father and will you please give him this envelope."

Back went the children through the biting cold, and burst into the house again. Avrom Itsik opened the envelope, and the smile left his eyes.

"Frume Leah has sent money for the *dreidle*," he said to Momme. His voice made the children feel that this was a most dreadful thing for Frume Leah to have done.

Back and forth across the room, Father walked with his hands behind his back. At last he took paper and a pen, sat down at the table, and wrote a letter. He wrote it in beautiful Hebrew letters with beautiful words borrowed from the Bible and other holy books. The letter began, "To the honored and esteemed Reb Nisan, learned in the *Torah,* and his pious wife Frume Leah, blessed among women." It explained that Father made *dreidlach* only to delight the hearts of the children, not for the sake of a reward. The *dreidle* was a small thing. He hoped that they would do him the honor to accept it as a gift, and that their grandson—may the Highest One grant him long life and blessing—would use it, and find pleasure in the festival.

Father put the letter into an envelope, and gave it to Goldie, together with the envelope they had brought from Frume Leah. Again the children set out for the big house off the square.

This time Frume Leah herself opened the door. She looked in surprise at Kezele and the little sisters. When Goldie handed her the two envelopes she seemed even more surprised.

"Come in! Come in!" she said, and she pinched Kezele's cheeks, and led the children into the big sitting room off the hallway.

Near the window was a *Hanukah* lamp such as the children had never before seen, a silver lamp that burned, not candles, but *oil* like the lamp in the Holy Temple. While the children marveled at the lamp, and ate the thin sugar-sprinkled cookies Frume Leah urged on them, Reb Nisan considered Father's letter.

Then he sat down at the big table, and wrote an answer. The letters he formed were even more beautiful than Father's, for Reb Nisan was a scribe. He, too, chose beautiful words taken from the holy books. The meaning of the words was this: that Avrom

161

Itsik's *dreidle* was a work of art, a masterpiece. If he had lived in the days of the Bible he would surely have been among the wise-hearted who fashioned the Holy Tabernacle in the wilderness. He and his good wife thanked him for themselves and also for their little grandson—may the Highest One grant him long years.

As for the money, it was no more than a bit of *Hanukah gelt* for the children—may their good luck be as great as their beauty and may the Heavenly One watch over them. He hoped that Avrom Itsik would not deny them this pleasure, since giving children coins on *Hanukah* was a fixed custom of the season.

After the letter had been written, the children bundled up again. Reb Nisan dropped *Hanukah* coins into their pockets and put the letter into Goldie's hands. Frume Leah gave her a jar of goose fat to carry home.

"Tell Mother," she said, "that the roast geese give out so much fat it is impossible to use it all. I could make a Sabbath pudding oozing with fat on every weekday and fat would still be left over." She turned to Reizel, her eyes smiling. "She will save me from the sin of waste by using this. You know about the sin of waste, Reizel."

Again the door of the little house opened and in came the children talking excitedly about sugar cookies and goose fat and *Hanukah gelt*. Gadya jumped on them in welcome, almost knocking over the jar of fat. Father's smile returned as he read Reb Nisan's letter.

"*Nu,* Gittel, what are we waiting for?" he asked. "Here is golden goose fat. Potatoes are in the bin. The calendar says it is *Hanukah.* Get started with the *latkes.*"

"*Latkes! Latkes* in goose fat!" the children clamored. *Latkes* fried in goose fat were as superior to *latkes* in poppy-seed oil as the Sabbath is to a weekday.

Kezele dragged out the big iron frying pan. Father built a fire of turf under the tripod. Fayge and Esther peeled and grated the potatoes. Momme mixed the batter, enough for a big pancake for each of them, but none to spare. She could guess to a spoonful how much of a mixture would be needed.

Off came the white cloth from Frume Leah's jar of goose fat and soon the first pancake was sizzling in the hot fat. It covered the whole bottom of the pan. The children stood by watching and sniffing, each with an earthenware plate in hand. The first pancake, of course, went to Father. Kezele got the second. He sat down on a low stool to enjoy it. Teppele watched him bite into its crisp brownness. His teeth left a little scallop at the edge, as snowy white as the teeth.

"Lend me a bite," Teppele begged. "I'll give it back to you when I get my *latke.*"

Kezele held up his pancake obligingly. Teppele

163

sank her teeth into the soft whiteness. "M-m-m!" Now, Reizel begged for a bite. Then Tseppele and the others. Esther didn't ask. But the sisters held the pancake to her mouth and before she knew it, she too had taken a taste. Kezele looked ready to cry when his pancake came back to him. Only the middle part was left. But by this time Tseppele had *her* crisp pancake. She returned Kezele's bite. She lent a bite to each of the others. Now came Teppele's turn. She had two bites to give back and four to lend.

"Wouldn't it be a good idea to give back the bites, but not lend any more?" Teppele suggested.

The children shouted her down. "Greedy! Selfish! It's not fair!" So Teppele's pancake, too, went the rounds.

All the while Father sat back in his chair enjoying the warmth and the good smells, and listening to the bargaining of the children.

"*Nu,* Gittel," he stid, "who said we need Rothschild's money? In this family we do business with bites."

Momme went on with the frying.

Esther's pancake was ready now. Momme turned it into her plate, crisp and golden. The children eyed it greedily. Esther owed bites to them all.

At that moment the door opened and in came Dena.

"Oh!" said Teppele. She knew what was going to happen. It did.

"You are just in time, Dena. We're having our *latkes,*" Esther said. "Take off your shawl." And she put the plate with the *latke* in Dena's lap.

"Esther is lucky," Teppele grumbled under her breath. "She doesn't have to give back any of the bites."

But Teppele didn't know what Momme was thinking. Momme's first thought was to give Esther her own pancake, now frying in the pan. But Esther might not take it. Besides, it was such a little pancake. A bolder thought came to Momme. God had been good. A full jar of goose fat had come to them. She would pour it out freely, and leave tomorrow and the day after tomorrow in God's hands.

"Go, fetch more potatoes," she said to the astonished Esther.

So the grating and the mixing and the frying began again. Each one was given another golden pancake. Even Gadya got one. And Esther had two. The bites that had been given up for lost were returned.

Truly it was a night of wonders and of benefits. And there were more wonders to come.

Feathers at Last

THE DAY OF THE fifth candle fell on a Thursday. Momme sat at the window, her hands busy with her knitting, her feet rocking Dovidel's cradle. She could see Hannah Rachel turn into the lane, carrying a plump goose under her arm. Its neck hung limp.

Now Momme, as you know, was a good and pious woman. Yet at that moment she coveted a goose. Not the goose Hannah Rachel was carrying. God forbid! Let her neighbor keep her goose and enjoy the holiday with her family. What Momme longed for was a goose *like* Hannah Rachel's. This was the season when the peasants drove their geese to market. The square was white with them.

Momme sighed. Her little daughters were growing up. Esther was already fifteen, almost old enough to marry. A fine young man had shown interest in her. And the pile of bedding in the corner grew no higher.

Dovidel awoke, crying.

"It is a good thing you are a son, Dovidel," Momme said as she lifted him from his cradle. "*Your* feather beds some other mother will provide."

How could Momme know that before the week of *Hanukah* had passed, Dovidel's sisters also would be

167

provided for? For Father's lucky *dreidle* was still spinning. It was spinning at that very moment on Frume Leah's kitchen floor.

Frume Leah had invited the children to her house to play *dreidle* with her little grandson, Yossie.

They sat in a circle, each with a pile of nuts to play with. Another pile was heaped in the center. The children spun in turn. Round and round went the *dreidle,* then toppled over on one side. Necks were craned to see which side. Was it the one with the letter *nun?* The spinner got nothing. *Gimel?* Ah, that was the lucky letter. The player gathered in the whole pile. Was it *Heh?* He took half the pile. *Shin* was the unlucky number. The player lost a nut. When the pile in the center was gone, each one gave up a nut of his own to make a new pile.

At first, Yossie hid behind his grandmother's skirts. Never had he seen so many girls at one time. But Reizel took out her *dreidle* and began spinning it on the back of a copper pot.

"Click, click, click, click, click," sang the *dreidle;* then it toppled over with a tiny clack.

Yossie looked out from behind his grandmother's skirts to see what was making the funny noise. Before he knew it, he was on the floor, spinning *dreidle* with the others. "Nothing!" "Half!" "All!" he shouted excitedly. He would not let his visitors go home until his grandmother had promised to take him to Kezele's house before the week of *Hanukah* was over.

On the afternoon of the eighth day Frume Leah kept her word. How excited the children were when Yossie and his grandmother turned down the lane! Reizel opened the door wide. Gadya leaped across the snowbanks to meet them. Soon the little ones were playing *dreidle* in the corner. They played for the small round nuts that were gathered in the fall and stored in a sack, above the oven.

Momme led Frume Leah to the table. It was covered with the crocheted cloth. Esther served glasses of tea, flavored with wild raspberry preserves. The preserves had been made for a time of sickness or childbirth, but this was a special occasion. Frume Leah sipped the tea slowly, commenting on the fine flavor of the preserves, the delicacy of the crocheted cloth, the beauty of Fayge's *mizrach*. Her quick eyes also noted the potato *Hanukah* lamp, but of this she said nothing.

Esther had gone over to the kettle to refill the glasses, when suddenly, for no reason one could see, Gadya jumped down from the top of the oven, skipped across the floor, knocking over Yossie's spinning *dreidle,* and climbed up on the pile of bedding in the corner.

"Meh-h-h," came his shivery bleat. "Meh-h-h."

Everybody turned. For the first time Frume Leah noticed the height—or rather the lack of height—of the pile of bedding. Her eyes narrowed in thought.

"Gittel," she said when the commotion had subsided, "have people told you that you are very like your mother, peace to her? She and I always spoke freely to each other. I will speak freely to you. A mother of daughters needs feathers. You have daughters, may they be blessed. I have a mountain of feathers. Let the girls help me with the plucking and we will divide the down between us."

"Do not think the favor is on one side," she added quickly. "You know the saying, 'All the shoemakers go barefoot.' I have long been wanting some new bedding. With the girls to help me, I'll have it."

Reizel's heart jumped as she heard Frume Leah's words. Elijah had listened to her! He was helping his little kid. *The wish of Momme's heart was to be fulfilled.*

She looked into Momme's eyes for some sign of the excitement that danced in her own. But Momme was not like Father. One could not tell from her face what was going on inside her.

"I'll be glad to have the girls help you, Frume Leah—and be thankful to you," said Momme quietly.

The excitement Reizel had restrained burst out when Frume Leah and Yossie left the house.

"Gadya, Gadya, you did it!" Reizel hugged the little kid until it bleated. "You've gotten Momme her feathers. There'll be a mountain of them. Frume Leah said so. It's like the prayer book says, 'a wonder and a saving act.' We ought to thank you, Gadya."

"Thank Gadya?" said Goldie. "You mean thank Father's *dreidle.* Kezele was right. Father does make lucky *dreidles.*"

The whole family was listening now, even Father, who came home early during the *Hanukah* week. Reizel was not to be put down.

"Of course Father's *dreidle* that he made for Frume Leah was a lucky one," she agreed, "but if Gadya hadn't run the wrong way and made me chase after him, I wouldn't have bumped into Frume Leah and she wouldn't have asked me to ask Father to make the *dreidle,* so there wouldn't have been one! Also, if Gadya had not jumped on the bedding, Frume Leah wouldn't have thought about feathers. So we have to thank Gadya for them," she concluded triumphantly.

"No, Reizel." Momme joined in the conversation. This was a matter which she felt had to be made clear. "It is God whom we must thank."

But Father, too, had something to say. "Gittel, did you never hear the saying, 'If God wills it, a broom shoots'? If God wills it, a kid can provide feathers."

Reizel heard him in astonishment. Father was standing up for her kid. Father was saying that Gadya could have brought the feathers. This was the greatest wonder of all.

Reizel flew across the room and flung her arms around Father.

So it came about that two nights a week during the rest of the long winter, Momme's daughters trudged through the snow to Frume Leah's kitchen.

There they sat at a deal table with fire pots under their feet, their quick fingers stripping and sorting the goose feathers. Into one pile went the small feathers, into another pile the down, into a third the sticks. Frume Leah always had a treat for them, bread spread with goose fat and onions, a slice of sausage, a piece of smoked goose, a little extra something for Reizel to carry back to Gadya.

What if the girls returned home with feathers caught in their braids and down powdering their hair! Momme did not mind. Down could be washed out with hot water and green soap; but the pile of feathers in the big ticks rose higher and higher, almost to the ceiling.

Reizel's heart danced whenever she looked at it. The wish of Momme's heart had been fulfilled.

A Crown for Esther

SPRING HAD ARRIVED, but had not yet decided whether to stay. One day the snow turned into slush, the next day into ice. *Purim,* the Feast of Esther, was at hand.

"Business has been better of late," Father said to Momme. "Make this *Purim* a real holiday, Gittel."

Purim was not one of the important holidays like *Pesach* or *Shevuos* or *Sukkos,* but it was the jolliest one in the year. On *Purim,* when the scroll of Esther was read, one could be noisy even in the synagogue. It was the *duty* of children to be noisy.

Rash, rash, rash, dr-i-r-r!

Wooden rattlers whirled, feet stamped each time the name of the villain, Haman, was mentioned. Haman, you remember, was the wicked prime minister who plotted to destroy the Jews, "young and old, women and children in one day." It had all happened long ago in Persia in the days of Queen Esther and her good cousin Mordecai.

One had to listen to the reading very carefully not to miss a single Haman. One also had to be careful not to whirl in the wrong place. It would be dreadful to make a mistake and boo Queen Esther. Esther was so beautiful that Ahasuerus, King of Persia, chose her from among all the maidens of the land to be his queen. Momme said that her beauty was the inner kind, that outwardly she was just average. But Reizel was sure that Momme must be mistaken. Esther *had* to be beautiful. Everybody agreed that she was brave. Think of going before the king to plead for your people's life when you knew that the guards would cut off your head unless the king raised his scepter. Reizel could recite Esther's exact words. "*So will I go in to the King, which is not according to the law, and if I perish, I perish.*"

Of course, Esther didn't perish. The king raised his scepter just in time. "What is your wish, my queen?" he said to her. "I will grant it to you, even if it be half my kingdom." So everything ended happily. The wicked Haman was hanged and the Jews had "light and joy, gladness and honor," and now they all had *Purim* for "joy and feasting and sending portions to one another."

Momme began preparing the "portions" the day before *Purim,* special breads and cakes and sweets: three-cornered Haman-pockets, filled with honeyed poppy seeds; *taiglach,* little balls of dough, boiled in honey; ginger-stick candies; carrot candies. Everybody helped. There were nuts to crack, poppy seeds to pound, raisins to cut, bowls to scrape. Teppele offered licks to everyone. *Purim* made her generous. Momme's cheeks were flushed and her eyes happy as she stirred and rolled and baked "like in the old days."

Now, on *Purim* afternoon, the children hurried through the snow and slush, delivering the "portions" in napkin-covered plates. At each house something was removed from the plate, something put in its place. Dena chose two ginger-stick candies from Reizel's plate, and sent back two diamond-shaped carrot candies. Hannah Rachel sent Momme a loaf of bread shaped like a crown. Momme returned a three-cornered loaf filled with poppy seeds. To the teacher, Reizel carried a package of tea, candies, and a huge Haman-pocket. Zissel, the teacher's wife, returned the plate filled with spicy chick-peas. Even Reb Lazer, "the old one" who lived by himself back of the tinsmith's shop, insisted on sending a portion to the family, an apple and two prunes. Momme had knitted him a pair of warm woolen socks.

The gift to Frume Leah took much thought. In the end Momme decided on a bowl of *taiglach,* a very special nut-filled kind which her mother had taught her to make. Frume Leah always said that no other *taiglach* could compare with them. But *nothing* could compare with Frume Leah's gift to the children. They could not believe their eyes when Momme lifted the napkin. Spread out on the plate were eight tiny toys made of candy: a cradle, a violin, a scroll, a bird, a little king, a wee horse, a goat, and a lamb. The children knew that such candies were sold in the big cities; but never had they seen any, much less received them. There were "ohs" and "ahs" and exclamations.

"Look at the darling violin. It has real strings."

"I choose the goat. It looks like Gadya."

"Esther should have the king."

Reizel presented it to her, bowing. "To Esther the Queen," the children chimed in. Their lips formed the words, "The name fits her," but they didn't say them out loud. Momme was too near.

The candies were distributed at last. Dovidel got the cradle, Kezele the horse, Teppele and Tseppele the lamb and goat, Reizel the scroll; Goldie, who was the sweet singer of the family, the violin. The

bird went to Fayge, because Faygele means little bird.

Teppele had a problem.

"I want to eat my lamb," she said plaintively.

"Then eat it," said Reizel.

"But if I eat it, I won't have it any more."

In the end she bit off one tiny hoof and took licks
at the rest. She was still licking when the guests arrived for the holiday meal. Besides Mume Bryna,
there were Todros and his mother. Kezele rushed to
the door to welcome them.

*A Crown for
Esther*

Not since Passover had the family enjoyed such a
meal. There was wine. There was a big braided holiday loaf, yellow with saffron, dotted with raisins.
There were cabbage-wrapped meat balls stewed in a
tangy sweet and sour sauce, and hot soup with

kreplach, little three-cornered, meat-filled pockets. There were cakes and sweets, and Zissel's chick-peas. There were songs with every dish.

Esther was pouring the tea when a timid knock sent her to the door. There stood a belated "portion bringer" with a covered dish in his hands. It was Buna Sasha's little son, Leib's cousin.

"It's for you," he said, handing Esther the plate. Out he ran without waiting for a thank-you or a treat. Esther lifted a corner of the napkin, then reddened, and replaced it quickly.

"What did you get, Esther? Let's see."

The children were out of their seats, clustering around her.

Esther held the napkin down tight.

"You're mean! We share everything with you."

"But I can't share it," Esther protested. Then, desperately, "All right. Look!"

She threw off the napkin.

On the center of the plate was a *golden crown,* carved out of a turnip.

No one had to ask who had sent it. They knew. Leib was in town again. A glance from Momme told the children there was to be no teasing.

"Come back to the table, everybody," she said. "Who ever heard of leaving before grace?"

Her eyes rested for a moment on Esther, then moved to the ceiling-high pile of bedding.

Reizel saw Momme's glance. She saw other things

all in a moment; Fayge's *mizrach* on the wall; up on the shelf, Tseppele's doll with the hat; Kezele sitting proudly next to Todros; Todros an honored guest; Teppele rubbing her stomach. How many good things had gone into it since the day they had surprised Momme with without-fish *with* fish.

"Things have gone better of late," Father had said.

"Everything has gone better since Gadya came," Reizel thought.

Suddenly she remembered that she had not seen the kid since morning. Where had he gone? She looked up at the top of the oven. Gadya wasn't there. He wasn't under the table. He wasn't playing with Dovidel.

Fear pressed on Reizel's heart. Elijah had brought the kid suddenly on *seder* night. What if he had suddenly taken him back!

"Gadya," she called out, panic in her voice.

"Meh-h-h!"

The answering bleat came from a corner, high up near the ceiling. Everybody turned. Gadya's head looked down from the top of the pile of bedding. He leaped, landing on a protruding feather bed. Another leap and he was on the floor.

Now Gadya stood up on his hind legs. His forepaws swayed. His tail wagged. He was dancing as he had danced on the *seder* night, almost a year ago, when he first came to them.

Reizel, Goldie, Teppele, Tseppele, the whole family

formed a circle around him. Kezele drew Todros in. Round and round they danced, clapping hands and singing.

> *Hi didi dai dai,*
> *Hi didi dai!*

A song without words! a joy-filled song!

They stopped at last, breathless. Gadya dropped to his four feet, went over to Reizel, and rubbed his head against her.

Father looked from Reizel to the kid, to Reizel again.

"I wouldn't be surprised," he said, "if Gadya came from Elijah after all."

HERE ARE SOME OF THE WORDS
AND HOW TO PRONOUNCE THEM

The names:

Avrom Itsik	(Avrom It-sik)
Dovidel	(Do-vi-del)
Esther	(Es-ter)
Fayge	(Fay-geh)
Frume Leah	(Fru-meh Lay-a)
Gadya	(Gaad-ya)
Gittel	(Git-tel)
Goldie	(Gold-ie)
Kezele	(Ke-zeh-leh)
Leib	(Layb)
Momme	(Mom-meh)
Reizel	(Ray-zel)
Rivkah	(Riv-kah. Hebrew for Rebekah)
Teppele	(Tep-pe-leh)
Tseppele	(Tsep-pe-leh)
Yitzhak	(Yits-hak. Hebrew for Isaac)

These are some of the family's favorite dishes:

Bagel	A hard roll shaped like a doughnut.
Borsht	A sweet and sour soup made of beets.
Gribines (gri-be-nes)	Bits of fat rendered with onion.
Haroses	A mixture of grated apples, cinnamon, chopped nuts, and wine eaten during the home ceremony on Passover. It symbolizes the mortar mixed by the Israelites during the Egyptian bondage.
Knaedel (Knay-del) (plural—Knadlach)	Matza-meal balls or dumplings.
Kreplach	Triangular pockets made of noodle dough stuffed with ground meat.
Latkes	Potato pancakes.
Matza (Mah-tza)	Unleavened bread eaten on Passover.

Taiglach (Tay-glach)	Small cakes made of spicy balls of dough boiled in honey.
Tsimmes	A sweet stew containing carrots, meat, and potatoes.

Some everyday words:

Bimah	A raised platform in the synagogue with a table at the center at which the Torah scrolls are read.
Heder	Hebrew school. Literally, room.
Kosher	Ritually correct.
Lamed	A letter of the Hebrew alphabet.
Mazel tov (Mah-zel-tov)	Good luck.
Mitzvah	A commandment; a deed pleasing to God.
Mizrach	The East. Also refers to a picture or verse hung on the eastern wall to indicate the direction of Jerusalem.
Mommele	"Little mother."
Mume	Aunt.
Rebbi (Reb-beh)	Teacher.
Rebbitzin	Wife of the Rabbi.
Sefer Torah (Say-fer To-rah)	A scroll in which the Five Books of Moses are written down.
Tallis (tah-lis)	A shawl with fringes on the corners, worn by men during prayers.
Talmud (Taal-mud)	Books containing the teachings of the ancient rabbis.
Tefillin (te-fillin)	Small leather cubes containing verses from the Bible, worn by men during the morning prayers.
Torah	The Five Books of Moses. Also refers to the entire Bible and the religious teachings of the rabbis.
V'yoh!	Giddy-ap!
Yad	A pointer shaped like a tiny hand, used when reading in the Torah scroll.

Festivals and fast days. The lunar or moon calendar told the family when each holiday was to come.

SHABBOS (Shaa-bos)	The Sabbath; observed on the seventh day of the week, beginning at sundown on Friday and concluding at sundown on Saturday.
Kiddush	Prayer for the sanctification of the Sabbath and holidays.
PESACH (Pay-sach)	The festival of Passover commemorating the exodus from Egypt.
Avodim Hayeenu	"Slaves were we." Part of the service on Passover Eve.
Had Gadyah	An only kid. The title of a song sung at the home service on Passover.
Haggadah	Book containing the home service for Eve of Passover.
Ma-nish-ta-nah ha-lai-lah ha-zeh mi-kol ha-lei-los	"Wherefore is this night different from all other nights?" Opening words of the four questions asked by the youngest son at the home service on Passover.
Pesachdig (Pay-sach-dig)	Pertaining to Passover.
Seder (Say-der)	The home service for the Eve of Passover.
Zuz (plural—Zu-zim)	A small coin.
SHEVUOS (She-voo-os)	The Feast of Weeks, commemorating the giving of the Ten Commandments at Mount Sinai. Synagogues and homes are adorned with green branches and grasses.
TISHA B'AV	The ninth day of the Hebrew month of Av: a fast day commemorating the destruction of the First Temple in 586 B.C.E. and the Second Temple on the same day in 70 C.E.
ROSH HASHONAH	The New Year: A solemn Fall festival.

185

Shofar	Ram's horn blown in the synagogue on the New Year.
YOM KIPPUR	Day of Atonement: devoted to fasting and prayer. The most solemn day in the Jewish year.
SUKKOS	Tabernacles; a joyful festival of thanksgiving commemorating God's protection of the children of Israel on their journey from Egypt to the Promised Land.
Sukkah	A temporary hut covered with green boughs used for meals, prayer, and study during Sukkos.
SIMCHAS TORAH	Rejoicing in the Torah (God's Law); the festival on which the reading of the Five Books of Moses is completed and begun again.
HANUKAH	The Feast of Lights or Festival of Rededication commemorating the victory of the Maccabees.
Dreidle (Dray-dle) (plural—Dreidlach)	A four-sided top spun on Hanukah. Each side is inscribed with a Hebrew letter.
Gelt	Money.
Nes godol hoyoh shom	"A great miracle happened there." The letters on the Hanukah top are taken from the initials on these four words.
PURIM	The Feast of Lots celebrating the events in the Book of Esther.

'Each second we live is a new and unique moment of the universe, a moment that will never be again...And what do we teach our children? We teach them that two and two make four and that Paris is the capital of France.

When will we also teach them: do you know who you are? You are a marvel. You are unique. In all the years that have passed, there has never been another child like you. And look at your body – what a wonder it is! Your legs, your arms, your clever fingers, the way you move. You may become a Shakespeare, a Michelangelo, a Beethoven. You have the capacity for anything. Yes, you are a marvel. And when you grow up, can you then harm another who is, like you, a marvel? You must cherish one another. You must work – we must all work – to make this world worthy of its children.'

Pablo Casals

A famous Spanish musician, also noted for his humanitarian beliefs.

(1876 - 1973)

I'm Hip-hop, the rapping rabbit from a starship far away,

It looks so good down here on Earth, I think I'm going to stay.

I just love this planet and you human beings too,

And I've bounced across five galaxies to have a word with you...

LIFE EDUCATION

My Wonderful Body

Written by
Alexandra Parsons

Illustrated by
Ann Johns, John Shackell, Paul Banville and Stuart Harrison

W
FRANKLIN WATTS

BY ARRANGEMENT WITH
LIFE EDUCATION INTERNATIONAL
LONDON • NEW YORK • SYDNEY

© Franklin Watts 1996
Text © Life Education/Franklin Watts

Franklin Watts
96 Leonard Street
London
EC2A 4RH

Franklin Watts Australia
14 Mars Road
Lane Cove
NSW 2006
Australia

ISBN: 0 7496 2364 0
10 9 8 7 6 5 4 3 2 1
Dewey Decimal Classification 612

Edited by: Helen Lanz
Designed by: Sally Boothroyd
Commissioned photography by:
Peter Millard
Illustrations by: Ann Johns,
John Shackell, Paul Banville
and Stuart Harrison
**Consultant for anatomical
illustrations:** Dr. Micheal Redfern

A CIP catalogue record for this book is
available from the British Library.

Printed in Italy

Acknowledgements:
Commissioned photography by Peter Millard:
5; 9; 10 (both);12; 16; 21.
Researched photographs: Sally Boothroyd 7;
Bruce Coleman 15; Bubbles 11, 18.
Artwork: all cartoons of 'alien' by Stuart
Harrison. Other cartoon illustrations by Ann
Johns: cover; title page; 7 (all); 8 (right); 9 (left); 13
(right middle); 17 (bottom right);19 (centre); 20
(all); 21 (all): John Shackell: contents page; 4 (all);
13 (left middle); 14 (all); 15 (all); 17 (centre); 18.
Anatomical illustrations by Paul Banville: 5 (all); 6;
8 (left); 9 (top right); 10 (both); 12; 16.

Franklin Watts and Life Education International
are indebted to Vince Hatton and Laurie Noffs
for their invaluable help.

Franklin Watts would like to extend their special
thanks to all the actors who appear in the Life
Education books (Key Stage 1):

Calum Heath   Jade Hoffman
Frances Lander   Karamdeep Sandhar

Contents

My outside . . . .

Your body is a wonderful piece of living machinery.
If you look after it properly, it will last you a lifetime.

LOOKING AFTER A CAR

INSTRUCTIONS ▶
Feed with interesting programmes.
Always follow the instructions. Don't use the keyboard with sticky fingers.

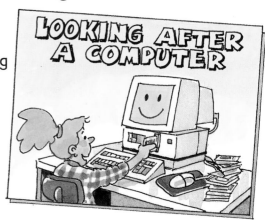

LOOKING AFTER A COMPUTER

▲ INSTRUCTIONS
Feed with oil, petrol and water. Take to the garage if it goes wrong. Drive carefully.

Super skin facts

☺ *Every 50 days you get a new top layer of skin.*

☺ *Skin colour depends on where your ancestors lived. Long, long ago, people who lived in sunny places developed dark skin to protect themselves from the burning rays of the sun. People who lived in cold countries had pale skin. Now many people's skin colour is somewhere in between.*

LOOKING AFTER A BODY

◀ INSTRUCTIONS
Feed the body with fresh food, fresh air and plenty of water. Feed the brain with plenty of interesting things. Take to the doctor if it gets sick. Give it lots of love and affection. Rest when tired. Exercise regularly.

Your body's completely covered in skin.

It keeps the outside out and your insides in!

Do yourself a favour, keep your skin clean,

Jump in the bath not the washing machine!

8

Look in the mirror and what do you see?

You've got a head, two bright eyes, a nose to smell, two ears to hear, a mouth for talking and eating and a neck that joins your head to your chest.

You've got shoulders to join your arms to your body, two arms with elbows so they can bend.

Two wrists so your hands can move, two hands, eight fingers and two thumbs.

You've got a chest, a waist, a tummy and a bottom.

You've got two hips to join your legs to your body, two thighs, knees with kneecaps so your legs can bend, two calves, two ankles so your feet can move.

And finally, you've got two feet and ten toes.

What's a body made of?

It is made up of tiny units called cells that stick together. Different cells make up the different parts of your body, so blood cells make blood, bone cells make bone, nerve cells make nerves and skin cells make skin.

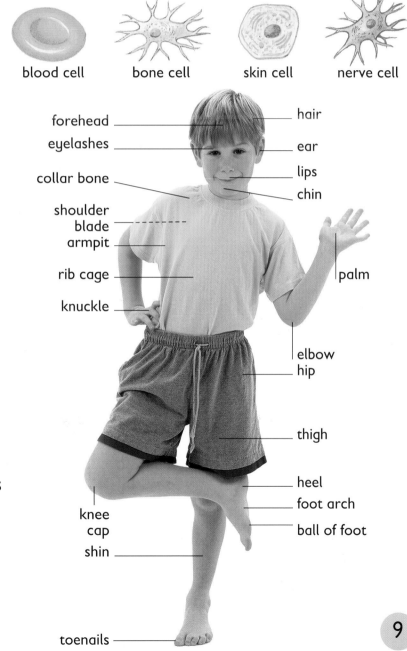

blood cell   bone cell   skin cell   nerve cell

forehead — hair
eyelashes — ear
collar bone — lips
chin
shoulder blade —
armpit —
rib cage — palm
knuckle —
elbow
hip
thigh
heel
foot arch
knee cap — ball of foot
shin —
toenails —

9

My bones . . . .

Your bones hold you up, give you your shape and protect your insides. Without bones, your body would be a big wobbly blob.

☆ Your skull protects your precious brain.

☆ Your spine is hollow! Inside the protective tunnel of your spine is a bundle of very important nerves, which carry messages from your brain to all parts of your body.

☆ Your rib cage protects your heart and lungs.

☆ Your breast bone holds your ribs together at the front. Your spine holds them at the back.

☆ Your hip bone is shaped like a bowl. It is actually made of eleven bones joined together.

☆ Your rib bones are thin and springy.

☆ Your arm and leg bones are long and thin.

☆ Over half of all the bones in your body are in your hands, wrists, feet and ankles.

Bones keep your insides
safe and sound.
Bones keep you upright,
standing your ground.
Each bone is different,
specially made,
From your little finger
to your shoulder blade.

Bone up on some facts

☺ The smallest bone in the body is a little bone inside your ear. It is about the size of a pea.

☺ The biggest bone in anyone's body is the thigh bone.

☺ When fully grown, everybody has 206 bones. Each bone is different. They all have different jobs to do.

Broken bones

Your bones are strong, but light. Children's bones are growing all the time. If a bone gets broken, it will mend itself (as long as the bits have been put back in the right place!). Children's bones mend faster than grown-ups' bones.

Poor Jess broke her wrist. She wore her plaster cast for two weeks.

This giraffe has seven neck bones, the same number as you do. But, as you might expect, the giraffe's neck bones are quite a bit longer than yours.

Slugs have no bones at all, nor do insects. Insects often have hard, shiny skin to protect their insides.

11

My muscles . . . .

Your body wouldn't be much use to you if you couldn't move it. And that is why you've got muscles. Muscles are like thick elastic bands and they are everywhere! You've got tiny muscles in your eyelids so you can blink, and big strong muscles in your legs so you can run and jump.

Muscles in the body

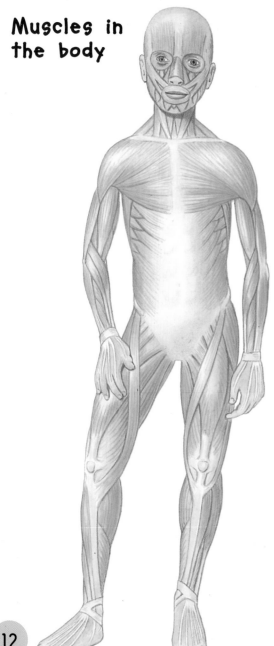

◄ Pull a silly face! You are using your face muscles.

See how many movements you can make with your arms! You are using your arm, upper back and upper chest muscles. ▶

◄ Pick up a pencil! You are using your hand and wrist muscles.

Breathe deep! ▶ You are using the muscles between your ribs and your tummy muscles.

◄ Bend over! You are using your back and tummy muscles.

◀ Jump up high! You are using your leg and foot muscles.

▲

Blink! You are using your eye muscles.

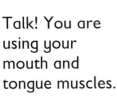

Talk! You are using your mouth and tongue muscles. ▶

How muscles work

Muscles can only pull, they can't push. So muscles work in pairs. When you bend your arm the top muscle pulls, and the bottom muscle stretches. Then when you straighten your arm, the bottom muscle pulls, and the top one stretches.

Muscle fuel

Muscles need energy so they can keep pulling and stretching for you. They get their energy from good, healthy food like vegetables and fruit. The more you exercise your muscles, the more they like it and the stronger they get.

Move that body, touch those toes,

Stamp that foot and wrinkle that nose.

Hear what I say, get mo–bil–ised,

Eat good food and ex–er–cise.

13

My heart and lungs . . . .

Cells in your body always need to repair and replace themselves. To do this they need two things: food and oxygen. Oxygen is a gas in the air we breathe. When we breathe in, thousands of tiny blood vessels in the lungs pick up the oxygen and take it into the blood stream. The heart then pumps the new supply of oxygen in the blood all around the body.

When you breathe in, your lungs fill with air. Lungs are made up of millions of tiny air sacs. Each sac is surrounded by lots of blood vessels. These take the oxygen from the air in the sac, and pass it into the main blood stream. Breathe deep!

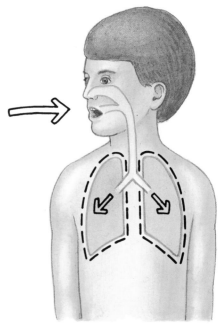

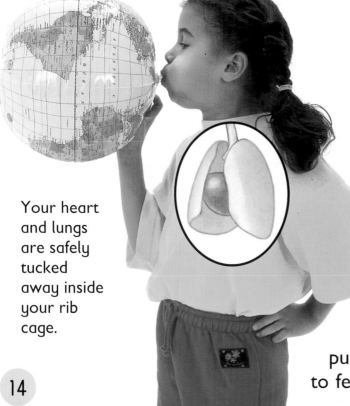

Your heart and lungs are safely tucked away inside your rib cage.

Your heart is a hard-working bundle of muscle about the size of a grown-up's fist. It pumps blood full of oxygen and other good things into blood vessels that are like a network all over the body. Blood that has given up all its oxygen comes back into the heart, and gets pumped around the lungs to fetch a fresh supply.

Hearts need exercise!

Your heart is made of a special kind of muscle that just keeps on beating without you ever having to think about it. (Isn't your body clever?) Like every other muscle in your body, heart muscle needs exercise to keep healthy. You can exercise your heart by moving around a bit every day, or cycling or skipping so your heart beats faster for a while. That's what a heart likes!

Here are some hearts and lungs having a really good time.

The air goes in and goes round and round,
Pumped by the blood to the heartbeat sound.
If a heart craves a little exercise,
Who are we to criticise?

Remember this!

☺ You have got nearly 100,000 kilometres of blood vessels snaking around inside your body.

☺ It takes about 20 seconds for a blood cell to travel right round the body.

☺ There are over 300 million air sacs in each lung. That's too many to count!

15

My tummy . . . .

It is very important to eat the right kind of food, because eventually the food you eat becomes part of you! Let's see what happens to this juicy apple.

First stop is your mouth, where your teeth chew up the apple into pieces small enough to swallow.

Your food pipe is lined with special muscles to push the little pieces of apple down to your stomach. This happens without you even realising it.

Next stop is your tummy – your stomach. The stomach is like a bag of muscle with a lot of strong chemicals sloshing about inside it. The chemicals get to work on the apple, and the muscles in the stomach wall crush the apple to a pulp.

By the time your stomach has finished its job, your apple looks more like apple soup.

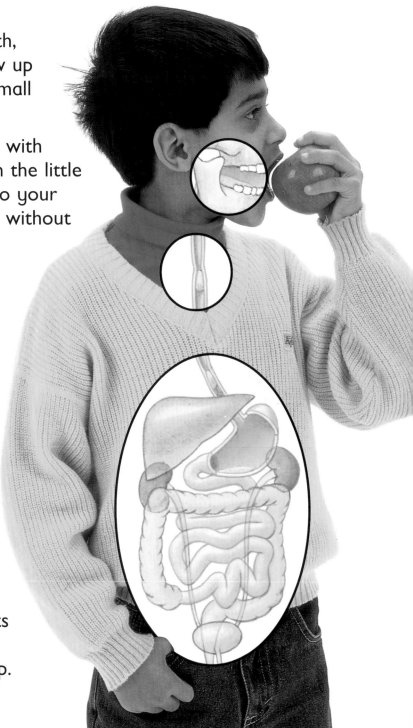

Next stop is the small intestine. This is a long, wiggly tube, about 6 metres long. Tiny blood vessels take in the nutrients, or goodness, the body can use, and pass them into the liver.

The liver sorts everything out. It sends good things into the blood stream to be delivered all around the body. This is to help repair worn-out bits and to build up your body and your brain. The liver works hard to change things that are not quite so good, like greasy foods and sweets, into something the body can use.

Your kidneys take liquid waste and water out of the blood stream. The liquid gets stored in your bladder. It comes out as pee.

The waste that the body doesn't want carries on its journey into the large intestine. The walls of this larger but shorter tube – it is about 1.5 metres long – suck up the water, so the waste becomes solid. It comes out as poo.

Hard to swallow!

☺ *If our digestive systems were straight instead of curled up inside us, human beings would be about 9 metres tall!*

☺ *Cows have four stomachs. They can sick up bits of chewed grass into their mouths and have another go at it. When the grass has nothing left to chew, it goes on down into the cow's intestines.*

Man, what a journey!
Boy, what a ride!
Fancy all that goin' on inside!
If my food's gonna end up as me,
I'll choose my meals more carefully!

17

My senses . . . .

You have five senses to help you understand what is going on around you: hearing, sight, smell, taste and touch. Special pathways, called nerves, run all over your body, a bit like telephone wires. Nerve endings in your ears, eyes, tongue, nose and skin send information from the outside down the wires to the brain. The brain can then work out what is going on and what ought to be done about it.

Nose: It's got a hint of this and a bit of that...

Brain: It's your favourite – chicken pasta. I'll send a message to your mouth to get ready for a treat.

Taste bud: Frankly brain, I don't like this at all. It's sort of bitter, and quite honestly it's rather puckered me up...

Brain: Spit it out, you idiot! It's not ripe and it might give us tummy ache!

Skin: Um.... not enjoying this much. Ouch!

Brain: It's that scratchy jumper again.... Just settle down, skin. You'll get used to it after a while.

Skin: Don't tell me what to do! You know how sensitive I am! I think I'll break out in a rash!

Your senses work hard just for you,

And they've got a lot to do.

It's their job to sort you out,

Tell you what the world's about.

It's sensational!

☺ Cats have better sight than we do. Foxes have much better hearing, and dogs have a brilliant sense of smell.

☺ The muscles that make your eyes focus move about 100,000 times a day.

19

My brain . . . .

Your brain is the cleverest thing about you. It is where your ideas and your feelings come from, where everything you have learnt ends up and where your memories are stored. It isn't much to look at – it looks a bit like a huge walnut. But that walnut is YOU!

Your brain is very delicate and is protected by your skull.

You're brilliant!

☺ The brain itself can feel no pain.

☺ The average brain contains 10,000 million brain cells. That's a lot!

☺ Messages travel within the brain at over 400 kph. That's fast!

Brains are so brilliantly clever,

Are brains amazing, or what?

If I give my brain a chance,

It'll be the best of the lot!

All parts of your brain have the job of sorting the messages sent from the five senses. Your brain is a huge store room holding everything you've ever learnt and the memory of everything that has ever happened to you.

The right side of your brain controls the muscles of the left side of your body. It also works out how to put things together – a skill you need for both music and maths!

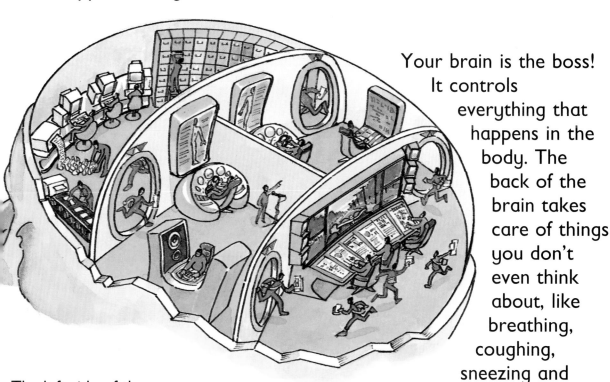

Your brain is the boss! It controls everything that happens in the body. The back of the brain takes care of things you don't even think about, like breathing, coughing, sneezing and digesting your dinner.

The left side of the brain makes it possible for you to speak, write and read. This control station also sends messages to the muscles on the right side of your body.

How does a brain keep going?

With your help! Brains need you to feed them well on healthy foods, give them plenty of sleep and stay away from alcohol, cigarettes and other drugs which mess up their control systems.

Thankyou!

21

My self . . . .

We know that we've all got 206 bones, 656 muscles, zillions of brain cells, a heart and a stomach and all the other bits that make up our bodies. So why aren't we all the same? Each one of us is unique because we are made up of a special combination of things we have inherited from our parents.

How babies grow

A baby grows inside its mother from a tiny egg. Inside the egg are all the special instructions that will make the baby grow up. These instructions are called genes. Half of the genes come from the mother and half from the father.

Fair hair
Freckles
Good at maths
Big feet
Love
from
MUM

Brown eyes
Long legs
Going to get
grey hair early
(sorry)
Good at telling
jokes
Love from Dad

Can you imagine what this little egg is going to look like, and what kind of a person she will be?

Brothers and sisters

Even brothers and sisters are different, because each one gets a different bundle of genes from their parents.

All the children got their father's hair. The eldest boy got his dad's mouth and his younger brother got his dad's sense of humour. The baby got her mother's calm nature.

22

You are unique!

So, you see, you are absolutely a one-off. There is no one else like you in the world! That makes you very special. You have got your inheritance, but now it is up to you to make something of it. Even if your parents are terribly fit, you won't be unless you eat well and exercise. And even if your parents are terribly clever, you won't be unless you fill up your **own** brain with your **own** knowledge.

Kids can make their own decisions about how they look after their bodies and their brains.

Your genes are your genes and my genes are mine.

You will be you, and you will be fine.

You will be fine because now you know,

It's **you** that decides how **you** will grow.

Gene genius

☺ Some genes are stronger than others. Brown eye genes are stronger than blue eye genes.

☺ You inherit the way you look from your parents, but your personality depends a little on your genes and a lot on the way you live your life.

23

My life . . . .

Who's in charge of your life? You are! Think of all the things you can do to keep your body fit and active. You only have one body, and a healthy body is much more use to you than an unfit one. And don't forget that hardworking brain of yours. It needs to be fed with new ideas, friendship, love and affection.

An unhappy body

A happy body

2+4

Your body's an amazing living machine,

You've got to get into a good routine.

Look after your body as you should,

You'll look great and you'll feel good.

That's my message, man, take it or leave it!

LETTER FROM LIFE EDUCATION

Dear Friends:

The first Life Education Centre was opened in Sydney, Australia in 1979. Founded by the Rev. Ted Noffs, the Life Education programme came about as a result of his many years of work with drug addicts and their families.

Ted Noffs realized that preventive education, beginning with children from the earliest possible age all the way into their teenage years, was the only long-term solution to drug abuse and other related problems, including violence and AIDS.

Life Education pioneered the use of technology in a futuristic 'Classroom of the 21st Century', designed to show in an exciting way the beauty of life on planet Earth and how drugs including nicotine and alcohol can destroy the delicate balance of human life itself. In every Life Education classroom, there are electronic displays which show the major body systems including the respiratory, nervous, digestive and immune systems. There is a talking brain and wondrous star ceiling. And there is Harold the Giraffe who appears in many of the programmes and is Life Education's official mascot. Programmes start in preschool and go all the way through secondary school.

There are parents' programmes and violence prevention classes. Life Education has also begun to create interactive software for home and school computers as well as having its own home page on the Internet, the global information superhighway (the address is http://www.lec.org/).

There are Life Education Centres operating in seven countries (Thailand, the United States, the United Kingdom, New Zealand, Australia, Hong Kong and New Guinea).

This series of books will allow the wonder and magic of Life Education to reach many more young people with the simple message that each human being is special and unique and that in all of the past, present and future history there will never be another person exactly the same as you.

If you would like to learn more about Life Education International contact us at one of the addresses listed below or, if you have a computer with a modem, you can write to Harold the Giraffe at Harold@lec.org and you'll believe a giraffe can send E-mail!

Let's learn to live.

All of us at the Life Education Centre.

Life Education, UK
20 Long Lane
London
EC1A 9HL
United Kingdom
Tel: 0171 600 6969
Fax: 0171 600 6979

Life Education, USA
149 Addison Ave
Elmhurst
Illinois, 60126
USA
Tel: 001 630 530 8999
Fax: 001 630 530 7241

Life Education,
Australia
PO Box 1571
Potts Point
NSW 2011
Australia
Tel: 0061 2 358 2466
Fax: 0061 2 357 2569

Life Education,
New Zealand
126 The Terrace
PO Box 10-769
Wellington
New Zealand
Tel: 0064 4 472 9620
Fax: 0064 4 472 9609

Useful words

Air sacs Tiny compartments in your lungs that fill with air when you breathe in.

Blood stream The blood flowing round your body.

Blood vessels The long, thin tubes that your blood flows through. You have blood vessels going to every part of your body.

Cells Tiny units of living material that make up your body. There are millions and millions of cells in your body and different parts are made of different kinds of cells – you have blood cells, bone cells, brain cells, skin cells and so on.

Energy The power to do work. Your body gets its energy from food, water and oxygen.

Genes Genes are like messages inside cells. As a baby grows inside its mother, the genes tell the cells what features the baby will have – what colour its eyes will be, how big its ears will be and so on. Half your genes are from your mother and half from your father.

Nerves Tiny cells that carry messages around your body to and from your brain. There are special nerve pathways all over your body carrying information and sending messages to help you make sense of the world around you.

Nutrients The good things in food which your body uses to build itself up.

Oxygen A gas in the air which your body needs to live and grow. Oxygen is taken into your lungs when you breathe in and is carried through the blood stream all around your body.

Taste buds Tiny bumps on your tongue that pick up flavours and let your brain know what they are.

Index

Useful addresses

Health Education Authority
Hamilton House
Mabledon Place
London WC1H 9TX
Tel: 0171 383 3833
Information leaflets on exercise, diet, smoking and health, plus a resource centre.

British Heart Foundation
14 Fitzhardinge Street
London
W1H 4DH
Tel: 0171 935 0185

Contact-a-Family
170 Tottenham Court Road
London
W1P 0HA
Tel: 0171 383 3555
Support for families who care for children with disabilities and special needs.

The Sports Council
16 Upper Woburn Place
London
WC1H 0QP
Tel: 0171 388 1277
Contact the information centre for any enquiries.

Dial UK (Disability Information and Advice Line)
Park Lodge
St. Catherine's Hospital
Tick Hill Road
Doncaster
DN4 8QN
Dial UK is the national organisation for the DIAL network of disability advice centres. Contact DIAL UK for details of local disability advice centres.

Australian addresses

People with Disabilities Inc
52 Pitts Street
Redfern, Sydney
NSW 2016
Tel: 02 319 6622
Tel: 1800 422015

Family Counselling
Tel: 1800 656 463

Aboriginal Health
73 Miller Street
North Sydney
NSW 2060
Tel: 02 391 9496